Awaiting oblivion

French Modernist Library

Series editors

Mary Ann Caws

Richard Howard

Patricia Terry

Awaiting

oblivion

(L'Attente l'oubli)

Maurice Blanchot *Translated by John Gregg*

University of Nebraska Press

Lincoln and London

Maurice Blanchot,

L'Attente l'oubli © Editions Gallimard, 1962.

Translation © 1997 by the University of Nebraska Press

All rights reserved   Manufactured in the United States of America

∞ The paper in this book meets the minimum requirements of

American National Standard for Information Sciences

—Permanence of Paper for Printed Library

Materials, ANSI Z39.48-1984.

Library of Congress Cataloging-in-Publication Data

Blanchot, Maurice. [L'Attente l'oubli. English]

Awaiting oblivion = L'attente l'oubli / Maurice Blanchot;

translated by John Gregg.   p.   cm.—(French modernist library)

ISBN 0-8032-1257-7 (cloth: alk. paper)

I. Gregg, John, 1954–   .   II. Title.   III. Series.

PQ2603.L3343A8513   1997   843'.912—dc20

96-273322 CIP

Publication of this translation was assisted by a grant

from the French Ministry of Culture

Contents

Translator's introduction

L'Attente l'oubli, published in 1962, occupies a special place in Maurice Blanchot's oeuvre, being his most experimental attempt to combine two very different, contradictory, and arguably incompatible modes of writing: narration and fragmentation. The uneasy alliance of these two forms may go a long way toward explaining why this work has received so little critical attention.[1] To the perplexing question of how to classify it as belonging to a particular genre, three essential responses can be given, following three avid and well-informed readers of Blanchot.

One could argue, as does Roger Laporte, that *L'Attente l'oubli* is "Blanchot's last narrative work."[2] In a review in the *Nouvelle Revue Française* on the occasion of the book's publication, however, Michel Deguy proposes a second solution, which is less categorical but more evasive than that of Laporte, by suggesting that *L'Attente l'oubli* occupies some sort of middle ground between philosophy and fiction. Deguy notes that "the beginning of the book appears to place it within the narrative tradition," but he also points to the work's aphoristic content, excerpts of which appeared, three years prior to its publication, in a festschrift in honor of Heidegger's seventieth birthday.[3] A third possibility is the one put forth by

Michel Foucault, who would prefer not to rely on an opposition such as philosophy and fiction in order to characterize the language of *L'Attente l'oubli*: "The distinction between 'novels,' 'narratives,' and 'criticism' is progressively weakened in Blanchot until, in *L'Attente l'oubli*, language alone is allowed to speak—what is no one's, is neither fiction nor reflection, neither already said nor never yet said."[4]

Foucault accurately identifies the three basic types of texts that make up Blanchot's oeuvre: the elaborate novels of the 1940s; the pared-down narratives (*récits*) of the late 1940s and the 1950s, which are comprised of moments that read like distillations of similar scenes found in his novels; and the critical essays that span his entire career. Moreover, Foucault correctly remarks that the trajectory followed by Blanchot's literary history has led him to the writing of works that escape generic classification and whose effect is to contest the boundaries thought to separate the activities of fiction and reflection, or critical reading and creative writing, into two clearly defined disciplines. The opposition between the discourses of philosophy and fiction that Deguy sees as the most salient feature of *L'Attente l'oubli* but that Foucault views as having been bypassed is, thus, not new or particular to this work. On the contrary, the tension between these two discourses resides at the very heart of Blanchot's entire literary enterprise.

With the possible exception of *Lautréamont et Sade*, his books of criticism are by their very nature fragmentary in that they are made up of essays that were first written for publication in periodicals. *Faux Pas* (1943), the most eclectic of these collections, contains nearly sixty articles that originally appeared in the daily *Le Journal des Débats*. The subjects of these pieces, inspired by the latest releases of critical studies, translations, poetry, and fiction, range from da Vinci's *Notebooks* and the French baroque poets to Giono's rendition of *Moby Dick* and Camus's *L'Etranger*. His second book of literary criticism, *La Part du feu* (1949; *The Work of Fire*, 1995), contains half as many essays as the first. In these longer pieces, originally published in *L'Arche* and *Critique*, Blanchot restricts himself to writers of the nineteenth and twentieth centuries—with the exception of Pascal—and in them there begins to emerge a kind of pantheon of exemplary writers to whom he will incessantly return in his discussions of the acts of reading and writing in years and books to come: Mallarmé, Kafka, Char, Hölderlin, and Nietzsche.

His next four books of criticism, *L'Espace littéraire* (1955; *The Space of Literature*, 1982), *Le Livre à venir* (1959), *L'Entretien infini* (1969; *The Infinite Conversation*, 1993), and *L'Amitié* (1971), are comprised almost exclusively of contributions he made to the *Nouvelle Revue Française* on a regular basis from 1953 to 1968. *L'Amitié* closely resembles *Faux Pas* and *La Part du feu* insofar as it is a heterogeneous collection of pieces written between 1950 and 1970. The other three titles, on the other hand, constitute the core of Blanchot's theory of literature, and although they are compilations of previously published essays, they possess a thematic unity that his first two collections do not: the books are divided into sections that have titles, and an implicit thread of argument ties these sections together in such a way that there is a sustained, progressive development throughout. *L'Entretien infini*, however, is distinguished from the two books that immediately preceded it by virtue of its stylistic variety, for it contains not only conventional essays but also dialogues and fragmentary texts.

In its multiplicity of forms, *L'Entretien infini* prefigures Blanchot's next (and last) two major books, which are fragmentary: *Le Pas au-delà* (1973; *The Step Not Beyond*, 1992) and *L'Ecriture du désastre* (1980; *The Writing of the Disaster*, 1986). Like *L'Attente l'oubli*, these works are unclassifiable, which is not to say, however, that no differences exist among the three. Because it possesses characters, a setting, and a story line (although these elements are reduced to a minimum), *L'Attente l'oubli* is undoubtedly more of a narrative work than the other two. *Le Pas au-delà*, however, also contains a narrative dimension, for it comprises not only aphorisms and lengthier prose passages of a reflective or philosophical bent but also dialogues and vignettes that could be excerpts from or preparatory sketches for his fiction. Moreover, specific allusions to other writers and thinkers are few and far between. *L'Écriture du désastre*, on the other hand, exhibits fewer modes of writing: there are only two dialogues and no narrative fragments. Curiously, given the wide range of topics discussed—from the science of etymology to the Holocaust, for example—and the large number of writers to whom Blanchot refers when discussing these subjects, this book comes across as a distant cousin of his earlier critical compilations, the difference being that the essay has been replaced by the condensed and more concentrated form of the fragment.

The setting of *Awaiting Oblivion* has been almost completely stripped of any references to concrete reality in favor of a minimalist universe: a hotel room sparsely furnished with a bed, an armchair, and a table is where everything takes place. What takes place has also been reduced to the bare essentials. The basic story line concerns the relationship between a man and a woman who spend an incalculable amount of time together talking as they alternate between waiting for something to happen to them that never does and vainly trying to remember something that may already have happened to them. The abstract setting, language, and plot of *Awaiting Oblivion* show how far Blanchot has come from, say, his portrayal of the panic-stricken city in his third novel, *Le Très-Haut* (1948; *The Most High*, 1996), which abounds in characters, dramatic situations, and allegorical storytelling.

In this story of an anonymous encounter between a man and a woman in a hotel room, Blanchot dramatizes his version of literary creation; of all his books, this is the one that approaches most closely what he maintains is the unreachable limit of the journal of a work in progress. The "essential solitude" of the writer who has penetrated into the undetermined milieu of the space of literature involves him in a rapport with alterity. Although the narrator of *Awaiting Oblivion* is alone, his writing has the effect of filling his room with voices that belong to many different beings, and it implicates him in a relation with alterity that is played out in the texts of the dialogues between his alter ego, the male lead, also a writer, and a woman, the mysterious, unknowable, unseizable figure of the *dehors*, the outside.

Although his description of the room serves as the point of departure of the relationship of the two interlocutors, what she really expects of him is that he write their story "that she would make it his obligation to carry through to the end and that must have as its outcome its progressive movement toward a goal." Both the characters (and the reader) assume that the story will lead somewhere, to a new awareness that they will reach after passing through preliminary evolutionary stages. No such destination is reached, however, and we wait in vain for something to happen to them. Daniel Wilhem suggests that the real "action" takes place elsewhere: "Discourse makes neither the event of waiting nor that of forgetting present; it does not turn such an event into an actual episode that is or can be named. This event is undoubtedly nothing other than what happens to discourse itself."[5] Whatever transpires in this story does so with respect to the language the characters speak, not to their lives, and if anything can be said to take place (albeit recurrently, not as a unique event), it is the subversion of one form of speech by another, the emergence of the language of passivity, which the language of power carries within itself but cannot contain indefinitely. Exactly what does happen in *Awaiting Oblivion*? Nowhere else is the "event" presented more succinctly than in the third fragment following the opening section: "It is not a fiction, although he is incapable of pronouncing the word 'truth' in connection with all of that. Something happened to him, and he can say neither say that it was true, nor the contrary. Later, he thought that the event consisted in this manner of being neither true nor false."

That the speech of neutrality, one that is neither entirely true nor entirely false, rises to the surface from deep within the language of negativity is the event recounted in *Awaiting Oblivion*. What the interlocutors say cannot be reduced to either of these states; their conversations express neither absolute truth nor utter nonsense. "Through the words a little daylight still passed." They never speak only the language of truth and comprehension nor only that of dissimulation and *non-savoir*. Meaning always manages to creep into the language of passivity, just as the murmur of excess negativity can always be heard beneath the surface of the language of discursive knowledge by whoever chooses to listen. Neither one silences the other once and for all.

The figures of speech that Blanchot utilizes most prominently to represent an experience that is, properly speaking, unrepresentable—the approach to/of the origin of a work of literature—are paronomasia and oxymoron. Paronomasia is understood here as the stringing together of words that are derived from the same root but that function grammatically as different parts of speech. An example, in the original: "Attendre, se rendre attentif à ce qui fait de l'attente un acte neutre, enroulé sur soi, serré en cercles dont le plus intérieur et le plus extérieur coïncident, attention distraite en attente et retournée jusqu'à l'inattendu. Attente, attente qui est le refus de rien attendre, calme étendue déroulée par les pas."6

This paragraph is circular in terms of both its content and the language of which it is composed. The key words of the passage are *attendre*, an infinitive; *attentif*, an adjective; *attente* and *attention*, nouns; and *l'inattendu*, a substantive formed from the past participle of *attendre*. Sentences made up of variants of the same word create the effect of being written by someone in a state of fascination, since they appear to be generated by the sonorous qualities of a language that feeds off itself (in this respect, note also the phonetic resemblance between *inattendu* and *étendue*) rather than by someone who views writing as an activity predicated on mastery. Oxymoron, the other trope used by Blanchot to express the ineffable, is also abundant throughout the text, in formulations such as "moving in immobility," or "at a distance without distance." Antistrophe, the repetition of words in inverse order, is another figure that Blanchot uses (albeit more sparingly than the other two) to create the impression of language written under the spell of fascination, as in the following examples: "They complain about eternity; it is as if eternity were complaining in them" or "Forgetting, waiting. Waiting that assembles, disperses; forgetting that disperses, assembles. Waiting, forgetting."

The fragments of this book fall into three basic categories. There are, first, those that are written entirely in the mode of direct discourse. Approximately one-eighth of the total number of fragments belong to this group, making it the smallest of the three. Composite fragments, so called because they are combinations of direct discourse and indirect asides, comprise roughly one-third of the fragments. The largest group, which numbers slightly more than one-half of the fragments, is completely narrative and contains no direct speech.

For the most part, the words of one or both of the interlocutors are uttered from a standpoint of ignorance. In their repetitious exchanges of questions and answers in the direct fragments, they attempt to arrive at a closer understanding of what is happening to them. A shift from direct discourse to objective narration, on the other hand, implies a change of perspective: the narrative passages that interrupt the bizarre and sometimes incomprehensible conversations are emitted from a point of view that is often superior to that of the two speakers. In most cases, the ignorance of the interlocutors in the direct discourse fragments is replaced by the more self-assured voice of someone who seems to be privy to secrets that the partners in the dialogues can only dream of knowing. The direct fragments, therefore, can be seen as primary texts in which the pulsating speech of passivity is clearly audible, whereas the intervening narrative fragments function as secondary texts, which tend to impose a limit on or put a temporary end to this speech by means of an act of interpretation. Put another way, the writer's rapport with his work is reenacted over and over again in the dialogues that take place between himself and the enigmatic visitor to his room. It is in their exchanges that the orphic protagonist reaches the point of closest proximity to the murmur that is at the origin of the language of his book. The narrative fragments, on the other hand, supply commentaries on this experience from a vantage point one step removed from the experience.

This distinction is, nevertheless, unstable. At times, the "primary texts" assume a voice of authority and superiority that is most often associated with the "secondary texts." Nor are the limits set by the seemingly self-assured voice of the readings invulnerable barriers: the language of the secondary texts is often contaminated by that of the primary text on which it is supposed to be a commentary. The authority of the commentaries is undermined by their own language, which participates in and helps perpetuate the aimless speech of passivity in spite of the pretensions to contain it.

Transgressive gazes of reading actually occur on three levels: the narrator-protagonist *je* tries (unsuccessfully) to assimilate the experience of his metamorphosis into the impersonal narrator *il*; *il*, like *je* always already divided, is split into two entities, the members of the couple, whom he fails to reconcile in his narrative fragments of observation; and the fissure within *il* is reproduced within the couple, previously the object of the narrator's analyses, when it becomes the observing subject of the experience of another couple.

The narrating subject has thus been split into six different entities. Rather than enabling the narrator to achieve a higher degree of self-presence, his writing has had a disintegrating effect, which removes him from a rapport of immediacy with his *moi*.

It is as if his foray into the space of literature has led him into a hall of mirrors whose concave and convex surfaces reflect back to him a multiplicity of images (*je* being one of many) that he is unable to recognize and assimilate as his own. Moreover, one has the impression that the phenomenon of refraction and doubling could go on forever. Blanchot certainly does his best to create this impression, but in the end he has to settle for three levels of doubling. Given the limits within which he must work, however, this is no insignificant achievement. He makes utmost use of the linguistic tools at his disposal—all the subject pronouns, all the tenses, two modes of discourse—by combining them in every possible way in order to portray the perpetual displacement of subjectivity with respect to itself.

Now that we have a summary understanding of the experience that the protagonist of *Awaiting Oblivion* undergoes, we may return to the question of how to classify this work in terms of a particular genre. I would like to suggest that *Awaiting Oblivion* is a rhapsody, in the sense that Blanchot himself attributes to this term in *L'Entretien infini*:

When commentators have not yet imposed their reign (as, for example, at the time of the epic), this work of redoubling is accomplished within the work itself and we have the rhapsodic mode of composition; that perpetual repetition from episode to episode, an interminable amplification of the same unfolding in place, which makes each rhapsode neither a faithful reproducer nor an immobile rehearser but the one who carries the repetition forward and, by means of repetition, fills in or widens the gaps, opens and closes the fissures by new peripeteia, and finally, by dint of filling the poem out, distends it to the point of volatilization.[7]

In this account of the rhapsodic style of composition that Blanchot sees at the heart of epic poetry, he accomplishes in one swift gesture a reversal of a commonly held notion. The opposition that he calls into question is that between creative and critical activity. Common sense tells us that the artifact precedes the critical appreciation of it. Blanchot disrupts this distinction, however, by placing the origin of criticism within the work itself. Thus, prior to a clear-cut distinction between creation and commentary, artists and critics, is the work of literature seen as a hybrid text. In the beginning is an incessant exchange between two irreducible, inseparable exigencies that renders possible their subsequent division into two separate and often opposed categories. Just as Homer doubles back to amplify or reflect further on the significance of an episode he has just recounted, the narrator of *Awaiting Oblivion* constantly casts orphic glimpses over his shoulder at the dialogues upon which he expounds in his indirect asides. Moreover, in doing so, he does not succeed in "filling in the gaps" by acceding definitively to a position of superiority with respect to what transpires between his characters/interlocutors. Instead, his activity distends his book "to the point of volatilization" in the longest fragment of the book.[8]

Blanchot's interpretation of the myth of Orpheus provides us with a clue as to how we might understand the title of *Awaiting Oblivion*. According to this account, Orpheus goes through three phases. He first undertakes his mission as a self-assured poet and savior who is prepared to wait patiently as Eurydice follows his footsteps in their ascent from the underworld. His attentiveness is then unexpectedly transformed into distraction, the absence of attention, when he becomes a dispossessed wanderer who is mesmerized by his own music, the resource that was supposed to protect him during his quest. Finally, he becomes oblivious to the divine edict not to look at Eurydice (the moment Blanchot designates as "inspiration") and thereby succumbs to the inevitable but indispensable sin of impatience: the temptation to extricate himself from his unintentionally self-induced trance and to make a last, desperate attempt to possess Eurydice in her nocturnal element.[9]

The same drama, in which a purportedly well-conceived act of power is inexplicably transformed into an impulsive act of transgression doomed to fail, is reenacted continually in *Awaiting Oblivion*. The narrator initially possesses the self-confidence displayed by Orpheus: all he has to do is describe the room and tell the story of the meeting of the man and the woman, that is, to use language as if it were solely an instrument of power. But the telling of the story is constantly waylaid by the interminable, repetitive, circular conversations of the characters. The narrator, the go-between who makes their rapport possible, is fascinated by their language to such an extent that he periodically feels the need to extricate himself from this relationship. The lesson that he has learned, thanks to his patient waiting for the woman's approach— that "it is her voice that is entrusted to [him], not what she says"—is thus necessarily and repeatedly forgotten whenever he surrenders to the orphic impulse to reread and comment on the interlocutors' conversations.

Furthermore, the narrator's transgressions fail to extricate him completely from his rapport with alterity and to bestow upon him the vantage point of superiority he seeks. He is toppled from that position whenever his discourse of power reveals itself to be contaminated by the spellbinding language of passivity over which it pretended to exercise control. An ebb and flow movement from personal subjectivity to impersonal spontaneity and back characterizes Orpheus's descent. The protagonist of *Awaiting Oblivion* gets entangled in this same vicious circle, the one that, according to Blanchot, the experience of literature holds in store for every writer.

Notes

1   For an extended discussion of *L'Attente l'oubli*, see the sixth chapter of my *Maurice Blanchot and the Literature of Transgression* (Princeton: Princeton University Press, 1994).

2 Roger Laporte and Bernard Noël, *Deux lectures de Maurice Blanchot* (Montpellier: Fata Morgana, 1973), 144. In passing, it is interesting to note that in a subsequent text on Blanchot, *Maurice Blanchot: L'Ancien, l'effroyablement ancien* (Montpellier: Fata Morgana, 1987), Laporte modifies his earlier position by saying that "*L'Attente l'oubli* [is] a transitional work [that] marks the end of [Blanchot's] novels and narratives" (66).

3 Michel Deguy, review of *L'Attente l'oubli*, *Nouvelle Revue Française* 118 (1962): 710.

4 Michel Foucault, "Maurice Blanchot: The Thought from Outside," trans. Brian Massumi, in *Foucault/Blanchot* (New York: Zone Books, 1987), 26.

5 Daniel Wilhem, *Maurice Blanchot: La Voix narrative* (Paris: Union générale d'éditions, 1974), 181–82.

6 Maurice Blanchot, *L'Attente l'oubli* (Paris: Gallimard, 1962), 20.

7 Maurice Blanchot, *The Infinite Conversation*, trans. Susan Hanson (Minneapolis: University of Minnesota Press, 1993), 390.

8 *Rhapsody* can also be defined as "a series of disconnected and often extravagant sentences, extracts, or utterances, gathered or composed under excitement; rapt or rapturous utterance" (*Standard College Dictionary*). One would be hard pressed to formulate a more concise and accurate characterization of the hypnotic and strangely beautiful language of this book.

9 For Blanchot's discussion of this myth, see the section entitled "Orpheus's Gaze" in *The Space of Literature*, trans. Ann Smock (Lincoln: University of Nebraska Press, 1982).

Awaiting oblivion

I

Here, and on this sentence that was perhaps also meant for him, he was obliged to stop. It was practically while listening to her speak that he had written these notes. He still heard her voice as he wrote. He showed them to her. She did not want to read. She read only a few passages, which she did because he gently asked her to. "Who is speaking?" she said. "Who, then, is speaking?" She sensed an error that she could not put her finger on. "Erase whatever doesn't seem right to you." But she could not erase anything, either. She sadly threw down all the pages. She had the impression that although he had assured her that he would believe her implicitly, he did not believe her enough, with the force that would have rendered the truth present. "And now you have taken something away from me that I no longer have and that you do not even have." Weren't there any words that she accepted more willingly? Any that diverged less from what she was thinking? But everything before her eyes was spinning: she had lost the center from which the events had radiated and that she had held onto so firmly until now. She said, perhaps in order to save something, perhaps because the first words say everything, that the first paragraph seemed to her to be the most faithful and so did the second somewhat, especially at the end.

He decided to begin again from there. He did not know her very well. But he did not need familiarity to get close to other beings. Was chance, which had assigned him to this particular room, responsible for their becoming so intimately involved with each other? In the meantime, others had occupied it, and she said that nevertheless she avoided them. Her room was at the end of the same hallway, a little farther down, at the place where the building began to turn. He could see her when she was lying out on the spacious balcony, and he had made signs to her shortly after his arrival.

He wondered if she was right to reproach him for his lack of faith. He believed her; he did not doubt her words. Seeing and hearing her, he was bound to her by a presentiment that he did not want to miss. What, then, was responsible for his failure? Why did she repudiate so sadly what she had said? Was she repudiating herself? He thought that at a certain moment he had done something wrong. He had questioned her too brutally. He did not remember questioning her, but that was no excuse; he had questioned her in a more urgent manner by his silence, his waiting, and the signs he had made to her. He had induced her to say the truth too openly, a truth that was direct, disarmed, irrevocable.

But why had she spoken to him? If he were to start seeking answers to this question, he would be unable to proceed any further. And yet it was essential as well. As long as he did not discover the correct reason, he would never be sure that she had truly said to him what he now did not doubt that he had heard—he owed this conviction to her presence, to the murmur of the words: the air continued to speak here. But later? He did not have to worry about later; he would not try to find any guarantees for another time. He would let her remain free. Perhaps he did not want to push her into other confidential revelations; perhaps, on the contrary, he secretly desired to keep her on this very tack. That appealed to him, but it also made him feel very uneasy. And so he discovered that he had other motives. Hadn't these motives altered, without his realizing it, what he had written with so much assurance? No, he said to himself. He experienced a vague feeling of despair when he thought of her despondent disavowal of what he had written. To be faithful, this is what was being asked of him: to take hold of this slightly cold hand that would lead him, by way of unusual meanders, to a place where she would disappear and leave him alone. But it was difficult for him not to wonder to whom this hand belonged. He had always been like this. He thought about the hand, about the person who had held it out to him, and not about the itinerary. Therein without a doubt lay his mistake.

While he gathered together the sheets of paper—and now she was watching him through curious eyes—he could not help feeling that he was bound to her by this failure. He did not understand very well why. It was as if he had touched her across the void; he had seen her for an instant. When? A few minutes ago. He had seen who she was. That did not encourage him; it suggested rather the end of everything. Period. "All right," he said to himself, "if you don't want to, I give up." He was giving up, but on an intimate note, in an utterance that, it is true, was not addressed directly to her, less still to her secret. He had been aiming for something else that was more familiar to him, that he knew and with which he seemed to have lived in joyous freedom. He was astonished to discover that it was perhaps her voice. It is the voice that was entrusted to him. What an astonishing thought! He picked up the sheets of paper and wrote, "It is her voice that is entrusted to you, not what she says. What she says, the secrets that you collect and transcribe so as to give them their due, you must lead them gently, in spite of their attempt to seduce, toward the silence that you first drew out of them." She asked him what he had just written. But it was something that she must not hear, that they must not hear together.

❖ He was looking at her furtively. Perhaps she was speaking, but on her face, no expression of good will with respect to what she was saying, no agreement to speak, a barely living affirmation, a scarcely speaking suffering.

He would have liked to have the right to say to her, "Stop speaking, if you want me to hear you." But at present, even saying nothing, she could no longer keep silent.

He understood quite well that she had possibly forgotten everything. That did not bother him. He wondered if he did not want to take possession of what she knew, more by forgetting than by remembering. But forgetting . . . It was necessary that he, too, enter into forgetting.

❖ "Why do you listen to me as you do? Why, even when you speak, do you keep listening? Why do you attract in me these words that I must then say? And never do you answer; never do you make something of yourself heard. But I will say nothing; be aware of this. What I say is nothing."

Undoubtedly she wanted him to repeat what she had said, merely repeat it. But never did she recognize her words in mine. Did I unwittingly change something in them? Did something change on their way from her to me?

In a low voice for himself, in a lower voice for him. An utterance that must be repeated before it has been heard, a traceless murmur that he follows, wandering nowhere, residing everywhere, the necessity of letting it go.

It is always the ancient word that wants to be here again without speaking.

❖ It is not a fiction, although he is incapable of pronouncing the word *truth* in connection with all of that. Something happened to him, and he can say neither that it was true, nor the contrary. Later, he thought that the event consisted in this manner of being neither true nor false.

❖ Poor room, have you ever been lived in? How cold it is here, how little I live in you. Don't I remain here only so that I can efface all the traces of my stay?

Time and time again, walking and always marking time, another country, other cities, other roads, the same country.

❖ He had often had the impression that she was speaking but that she was not yet speaking. And so he waited. He was, confined with her, in the great shifting circle of waiting.

❖ "Act in such a way that I can speak to you." — "Yes, but do you have any idea of what I should do to accomplish that?" — "Persuade me that you hear me." — "Well, then, begin; speak to me." — "How could I begin to speak if you do not hear me?" — "I don't know. It seems to me that I hear you." — "Why this familiar form of address? You never address anyone that way."* — "This is indeed proof that I am addressing you." — "I am not asking you to speak: to hear, only to hear." — "To hear you or to hear in general?" — "Not me, you have understood that well. To hear, only to hear." — "In that case, may it not be you who are speaking, when you speak."

And, therefore, in a single language always to make the double speech heard.

It was a kind of struggle that she was pursuing with him, a silent dispute through which she asked him for and gave him justification.

❖ And yet hadn't he cautioned her from the very first day, that day which was not yet quite the first one, when she had seemed to him so uncomfortable being there, surprised and almost irritated, waiting for him to justify himself while justifying her?

*The male speaker has shifted abruptly from *tu* to *vous*, which does not go unnoticed by his companion. She nonetheless continues to use the formal *vous* throughout this fragment. On many occasions, the characters address each other in the familiar form, although *vous* is used most of the time.

With his youthful vigor, he had not hesitated then to respond. It was a brilliant period when everything still seemed possible and when he threw caution to the wind, randomly taking note, always with sovereign rectitude, of the essential detail and entrusting the rest to his flawless memory.

❖ It is as if she had waited for him to give her a detailed description of this room that, however, she was occupying with him. Perhaps in order to reinforce the certainty that she was really there. Perhaps because she had the feeling that this description would conjure up this same room inhabited by someone else.

In this extreme point of waiting where for a long time what is awaited has served only to maintain the waiting, in what may be the last moment, perhaps the infinite one: man still among us.

To try to remain ignorant of what one knows, only that.

❖ What was he carrying on his shoulders? What absence of himself was weighing so heavily on him?

❖ He then tried to look at the room more out of idleness than interest: it was a hotel room. Narrow and long, abnormally long perhaps.

❖ When he understood that she was not trying to tell him how things had transpired—maybe she said this in addition to everything else—but rather that she was engaged in a cold, painful struggle against certain words that had been placed in her care, so to speak, and whose connection she strove to maintain with the future or with something that had not yet come about, nevertheless already present, nevertheless already past, he felt afraid for the first time. To begin with, he would know nothing (and he could see how much he had wanted to know); moreover, he would never perceive at what moment he would be on the verge of finishing. What a serious, frivolous existence with no resolution, with no perspective, would result; as for his relations with her, a perpetual lie.

❖ The characteristic of the room is its emptiness. When he enters, he does not notice it: it is a hotel room no different from those he has always lived in, the kind he likes, in a modest hotel. But as soon as he wants to describe it, it is empty, and the words that he uses apply only to the emptiness. Yet with what interest she watches him when he says to her: here is the bed, there a table, over where you are, an armchair.

She imagined—at least this was his impression—that he had at his disposal a great power that he could have used to reach the heart of this truth that she seemed to have constantly before her without succeeding in making it real; but through an incomprehensible negligence, he refused to do anything with this power. "Why don't you do everything that you could?" — "But what could I do?" — "More than you are doing." — "Yes, probably more, a little more," he added lightheartedly. "I have often had this impression since I have known you." — "Be sincere: why don't you make use of this power that you know you have?" — "What kind of power? Why are you telling me this?" But she persisted with her calm obstinacy: "Acknowledge this power that belongs to you." — "I do not know it, and it does not belong to me." — "That proves that this power is part of you."

The voices ring out in the immense emptiness, the emptiness of the voices and the emptiness of this empty place.

❖ The words wear out in her the memory that they help her express.

In her memory, nothing except suffering that cannot be remembered.

❖ His desire to hear her well had long since given way to a need for silence whose indifferent background would have been formed

7

by everything that she had said. But only hearing could nourish this silence.

They both searched for poverty in language. On this point, they agreed. For her there were always too many words and one word too many, as well as overly rich words that spoke excessively. Although she was apparently not very learned, she always seemed to prefer abstract words, which evoked nothing. Wasn't she trying, and he along with her, to create for herself at the heart of this story a shelter so as to protect herself from something that the story also helped attract? There were moments when he believed this and sentences that made him believe this.

Perhaps, by proposing this story to him, she wanted only to destroy in him the will to express himself, to which she sought, at the same time, to reduce him.

❖ There must be no turning back.

❖ To wait, to make oneself attentive to that which makes of waiting a neutral act, coiled upon itself in tight circles, the innermost and outermost of which would coincide, attention distracted in waiting and returned all the way to the unexpected. Waiting, waiting that is the refusal to wait for anything, a calm expanse unfurled by steps.

He experiences the impression of being in the service of an initial distraction that would let itself be reached only when dissimulated and dispersed in acts of extreme attention. Waiting, but subordinated to that which could not allow itself to be awaited.

To wait seems to signify for her the relegation of herself to a story that she would make it his obligation to carry through to the end and that must have as its outcome its progressive movement toward a goal. The attention should be exerted, so to speak, by this narrative in such a way as to draw it slowly out from the initial distraction, without which, however—he senses it well—attention would become a sterile act.

To wait: what did he have to wait for? She manifested her surprise if he asked her this question because for her, it was a word that sufficed on its own. As soon as one waited for something, one waited a little less.

❖ The extraordinary pressure that discretion and the silent waiting exerted on him. For quite some time they had no longer been hoping to arrive at the end that they had set for themselves. He no longer even knew if she continued to talk to him about this thing. He was looking at her furtively. Perhaps she was speaking, but on her face, no expression of good will with respect to what she was saying . . .

❖ He would not do it. "If you do not do it, you will still do it." — "But is that what you desire?" — "Ah, you are not going to get out of it like that. If you do it, I will desire it." He reflected: "Perhaps I could have done it in an earlier time." — "When exactly?" — "Well, when I didn't know you." This made her laugh: "But you don't know me."

❖ "Yes." Does she really say this word? It is so transparent that it lets what she says pass through, including the word itself.

❖ "So, it happened here and you were with me?" — "Perhaps with you: with someone whom I cannot fail now to recognize in you."

From the outside, he would have liked for things to be better understood as they really were: instead of the beginning, a kind of initial void, an energetic refusal to let the story get under way.

Story, what does she mean by that? He remembers the words that had one day burst into his life. "No one here wants to get involved in a story."* An almost faded memory that, nevertheless, continues to haunt him.

*This sentence was originally uttered by one of the characters of Blanchot's *Au moment voulu* (1951; *When the Time Comes*, 1985).

❖ "I will do everything you want." But now that was no longer enough for her. "I am not asking you to help me; I am asking that you, too, be here and wait." — "What must I wait for?" But she did not understand this question. As soon as one waited for something, one waited a little less.

❖ "When I speak to you, it is as if the entire part of me that covers and protects me abandoned me and left me exposed and very vulnerable. Where does this part of me go? Is it in you that it turns against me?"

He senses that she is waiting for him to carry her far enough so that the memory can be remembered in her and expressed. This is what they do not cease to evoke at every instant.

Secretly before the gaze of everyone.

As if pain's proper dimension were thought.

❖ "All right," he said to himself while closing his eyes, "if you don't want to, I give up." He realized that she might have forgotten everything. This forgetting was part of what she would have liked to say to him. In the beginning, with his youthful vigor and brilliant certainty, he had reveled in this forgetting, which seemed to him at the time very close to what she knew, closer perhaps than recollection, and it is through forgetting that he sought to gain possession of it. But forgetting . . . It would have been necessary that he, too, enter into forgetting.

❖ *Act in such a way that I can speak to you.*

"What must I say?" — "What do you want to say?" — "That which, if I were to say it, would destroy this will to say."

She gave the impression, when she spoke, of not knowing how to reestablish a bond between her words and the richness of a preexisting language. They had no history, no connection with the past of everyone else, not even any relation to her own life or to anyone else's. And yet they said what they said with a precision that their lack of ambiguity alone rendered suspect: as if they had had a single meaning outside of which they would again fall silent.

The meaning of this whole story was that of a long sentence that could not be cut up into segments, that would discover its meaning only at the end and that, at the end, would find its meaning only as a breath of life, the motionless movement of the story in its entirety.

He started hearing to the side of what she was saying, and as if behind it, but in an expanse without depth, with no top or bottom, yet which was materially locatable, another utterance with which hers had almost nothing in common.

❖ *Act in such a way that I can speak to you.*

❖ The refusal with which she resisted him lay in her very docility. Everything was obscure, this he knew, cloudy perhaps, and her presence was linked to a doubt: as if she had been present only so that she could prevent herself from speaking. And then there were moments when the thread of their relations having been broken, she regained her tranquil reality.

Then he saw better what an extraordinary state of weakness she was in, from which she derived the authority that sometimes made her speak. And what about him? Wasn't he too strong to hear her, too convinced of the extensive meaning of his own existence, too carried away by its movement?

What was missing in what she said, in her simplest sentences?

❖ *Act in such a way that I can speak to you.* Is that what she really wanted? Was she sure that she would not regret it? "Oh yes, I will regret it. I already do." But, not without sadness, she added: "You will regret it, too." At which point, however, she remarked: "I will not tell you everything; I will tell you almost nothing." — "But in that case, it would be better not to begin." She laughed: "Yes, but the problem is that I have already begun now."

He has always known that there is nothing in all of this that cannot be expressed by the most common words, provided that he himself belongs to this same secret instead of knowing it and that he forsakes his share of light in this world.

He would never know what he knew. Such was solitude.

❖ "Give that to me." He listens to this injunction as if it came from him, addressing itself to him. "Give that to me." An utterance that does not resemble a request, nor does it really seem like an order; a neutral, white utterance that (not without hope) he feels he will not always resist. "Give that to me."

❖ He is at this moment engaged in an error from which he does not wish to exclude himself and which is only the resumption of his oldest errors. He does not even recognize it, and when he is told, "But this thought, it is always the same thought!" he is content to reflect and finally responds, "Not exactly the same one, and I would like to think it a little longer."

I can hear only that which I have already heard.

❖ He wonders if she does not remain alive so as to make the pleasure of ending life last.

❖ That he could leave: he knew that he owed his ability to stay to this assurance. But he felt that his leaving, which was something that could be accomplished most easily on a personal level, possessed on another level all the characteristics of a decision that could never be carried out. He would leave, but he would, nevertheless, stay. This was the truth around which she, too, was circling stealthily.

And sometimes, with an indifference that was already a kind of proof, he wondered if he hadn't reached this second form of his stay: he was there because at a certain moment, he had left.

He was forcing her to speak, he realized that now. He would close the room up almost immediately after she entered. He would put another room in its place, the same one, and just as he had described it to her, yes, just like it—he would not deceive her in this respect—only more barren on account of the very barren words, reduced to the space of a few names outside of which he knew she would never stray. How they suffocated together in these close quarters, where the words she said could signify nothing other than this confinement. Didn't she always say this and only this: "We are shut in; we will never again leave this place"?

It slowly, suddenly dawned on him: from then on, he would look for a way out. He would find it.

❖ And yet everything remained unchanged.

❖ The room is illuminated by two windows that form oblique openings in the wall a few feet away. Light comes in almost evenly all the way to a table, a massive, solid, black one. Next to the table, at the edge of the part of the room that is still very well lit, although the sun does not reach there, sitting up straight in a chair whose armrests she does not use, she is breathing slowly.

"Do you want to leave this room that badly?" — "It must be done." — "You cannot leave now." — "It must be done, it must be done." — "Only when you have told me everything." — "I will tell you everything, everything that you want me to say." — "Everything that you must say." — "Yes, everything that you must hear. We will remain together; I will tell you everything. But not right now." — "I am not preventing you from leaving." — "You must help me, as you well know."

❖ It is not true that you are shut in with me and that everything you have not yet told me separates you from the outside. Neither one of us is here. Only a few of your words have entered, and we listen to them from afar.

❖ Do you want to separate yourself from me? But how will you go about it? Where will you go? In what place are you not separated from me?

❖ If something happened to you, how can I bear to wait to know what it is so that I will not to have to bear it? If something happened to you—even if it happens only much later and long after my disappearance—how can it not be unbearable as of now? And, it is true, I cannot bear it completely.

❖ To wait, only to wait. Unfamiliar waiting, equal in all its moments, as is space in all its points; similar to space, exerting the same continuous pressure, not exerting it. Solitary waiting that was within us and has now passed to the outside, waiting for ourselves without ourselves, forcing us to wait outside our own waiting, leaving us nothing more to await. At first, intimacy; at first, the ignorance of intimacy; at first, instants unaware of each other existing side by side, touching and unconcerned with each other.

He tried, at times painfully, not to take her into account. She took up so little room. She remained seated, her back straight, her hands resting on the table in such a way that when he looked up, he could limit his sight of her to her idle hands. At times, he thought that she had gotten up and walked across the room. But she was there.

"You know everything already." — "Yes, I know everything." — "Why do you compel me to say it to you?" — "I would like to know it from you and with you. It is something that we can only know together." She reflected: "But don't you risk knowing it a little less?" He reflected in turn: "That doesn't make any difference. You must say it once, one time; I have to hear you say it." — "If I say it once, I will say it always." — "Yes, that's it, always.

"I do not want to know it. I want you to say it to me so that I will not have to know it." — "No, no, not that."

❖ He knew, and it seemed to him that she knew, that somewhere here there was a kind of void. If he examined this question with the patience that enabled him to eliminate without violence all irrelevant concerns, he would not hesitate to conclude that the void was located at a place that he could have situated had he been capable of applying his mind more seriously to the task. But it required too great an effort on his part to think about it and even to remember it. It was as if he had introduced inside his thought a form of suffering that, as soon as it was awakened, forced him not to think about it. And yet on that day, he went further. He imagined that if he could describe this room exactly, meticulously and not fleetingly, without taking into account his presence but rather by trying to distribute it around her presence, he would almost necessarily discover what was missing, the lack of which made them both dependent on something that at times appeared to him as threatening, at others as joyous, or as threateningly joyous. Naturally, he knew that he had become not very fond of looking at this room, but only since she had not stopped asking him, with silent insistence, to describe it to her over and over. Formerly, whenever he entered it, he had found it almost pleasant.

There was a point of weakness and distraction in him that he had to relate to everything that he thought and said, at the risk of committing what seemed to him to be the essential infidelity. Everything that he had written and had had to live through had been arranged and oriented, by an ill-perceived necessity, around this point like a capricious, shifting force field. What was this point? From time to time, he had approached it. He had persistently translated the astonishing discoveries of this approach. And each time he was ready to begin this movement again: against his will and yet willingly; not willingly, against his will only.

❖ He thought that he had learned patience, but he had only lost impatience. He no longer had either one; he had only their lack, from which he imagined that he was able to derive an ultimate strength. Without patience, without impatience, neither consenting nor refusing, abandoned without abandon, moving in immobility.

With what melancholy and yet with what calm certainty he felt that he would never again be able to say "I."

❖ We must always, with respect to each moment, conduct ourselves as if it were eternal and relied on us to become ephemeral again.

They always discussed the moment when they would no longer be here, and although they knew that they would always be here to discuss such a moment, they thought that there was nothing more noble about their eternity than to spend it evoking its end.

❖ Is there a door that he did not notice? Is there a smooth wall where two windows open out? Is there always the same light even though night has fallen?

❖ Express only that which cannot be expressed. Leave it unexpressed.

❖ Something negative helped her speak. He had the impression that in each of her sentences, she always made room for the possibility of finishing.

She worked visibly hard not to support everything she said with her existence. If it is possible not to stand behind what one says, not to endow words with any life or warmth, to speak at a distance from oneself and yet with the greatest passion, a passion without warmth and without life, then it was indeed she who was speaking now.

❖ What he had never asked her: if she spoke the truth. This is what explained the difficulty of their relations; she spoke the truth, but not in what she said.

And there had been that day when she had declared: "I know now why I do not respond to you. You do not question me." — "That is true; I do not question you as I should." — "And yet you question me constantly." — "Yes, constantly." — "That gives me too much to respond to." — "I ask, however, for very little; admit it." — "Too little for my life to be adequate to the task." She was standing almost beside him, looking straight ahead: "Naturally, if I were to die, you would not fail to call me back to life in order to make me respond again." — "Unless," he said smiling, "I die first." — "I hope not; that would be worse."* She stopped and went back as though to another idea: "I must be capable of knowing only one thing." — "As I must be of hearing only one thing. But we fear that it might not be the same thing. We take our precautions." I can hear only what I have already heard.

❖ "Do you have doubts about me?" She meant about her truthfulness, her words, her actions. But I sensed a greater doubt.

Ah, if only I could have persuaded myself that she was hiding something from me. "Do you have a secret?" — "You are the one who has it now, as you know." Yes, unfortunately, I knew that I had it, without knowing what it was.

And, to conclude, with fervor: "Could I have talked without stopping?"

❖ You must be careful: such a figure! Lawless, it is appearance, but it is as if it were attached to a particular point of this place, a point that it would make visible if your desire to see it did not push away all the rest.

The thoughts of the night, always more brilliant, more impersonal, more painful. Infinite pain and joy are constant, and, at the same time, tranquillity.

*This exchange succinctly summarizes what transpires in Blanchot's earlier narrative *L'Arrêt de mort* (1948; *Death Sentence*, 1978).

❖ "I would like you to love me only through that which is impassive and unfeeling in you."

❖ Hadn't she suggested to him from time to time that even if the description remained unfinished, it was always complete and lacked only their own absence? Whether this was cause for joy or alarm on her part was not known. "When we have left." Or simply: "When you are no longer here." – – "In that case, you will no longer be here, either." — "I will no longer be here, either."

❖ Two utterances clinging tightly to each other, like two bodies but having indistinct boundaries.

❖ Her good will was extraordinary. He questioned her, she responded. This response, it is true, said nothing more than the question and merely closed it again. It was the same utterance returning toward itself, and yet not exactly the same, as he was well aware; there was possibly a difference in this return, which would have taught him very much if he had been capable of recognizing it. Perhaps it is a difference of time; perhaps it is the same utterance slightly faded, slightly enriched with a singular meaning on account of this fading, as if there is always a little less in the response than in the question.

"All your words question me, even when you say things that are not related to me." — "But everything is related to you!" — "Not to me. I am here; that should be enough for you." — "Yes, that should be enough, provided that I can count on you." — "Don't you count on me?" — "I would if it were you." He was close to divulging to her what he had already sensed: where she was, there was an indistinct assemblage stretching to infinity and disappearing into the day, a crowd that was not a true crowd of people but something uncountable and indefinite, a kind of abstract weakness, incapable of presenting itself in any other way than in the empty form of a very large number. And yet whatever her relationship to the crowd was, she was never really engulfed by it, asserting herself, on the contrary, with a gentle authority that made her more present and more persuasive.

"I see everything that you have said around you, like a multitude into which you would be invited to let yourself be absorbed, a kind of weak, almost dreadfully weak thing." — "I sense that as well. Its movement is constant." — "Is what we say really that pitiful?" — "Pitiful, I'm afraid so, but it is my fault." — "It is our fault." — "Yes, yes," she says joyously, "it is our fault."

❖ Through the words a little daylight still passed.

❖ "When did he say that to you?" — "Did he say it to me?" — "He didn't tell you that he enjoyed being with you?" — "What a curious choice of words!" That put her in a good mood. "No, he never spoke in those terms." And with peculiar energy, "He did not enjoy being with me; he did not enjoy being with anyone." — "Ah, that is saying a lot. He lived on his own? He didn't like to see people very much?" And before she took the liberty of responding, he boldly formulated the question: "Why, then, did he remain almost the entire time with you?" She listened to this utterance, which she seemed to let settle beside her. She was motionless, and he wondered if she would endure being the center of such pressure for very long, but she more than withstood it, and to his surprise she may have said more to him than she had ever said before, and in a way that awakened in him a distant, painful awareness: "Yes, he remained almost the entire time with me."

He remained almost the entire time with her.

❖ The pressure of the city: from all parts. The houses are not there so that people can live in them, but rather so that there can be streets and, in the streets, the city's incessant movement.

❖ "We are not alone here." — "No, we are not really alone. Would we accept being alone?" — "Alone, but not each one for his own sake; alone in order to be together." — "Are we together? We aren't completely, are we? We're only together if we could be separated."

❖ "Are we together? Not quite, are we? Only if we could be separated." — "We are separated, I am afraid, by everything that you do not want to say about yourself." — "But also united because of that." — "United: separated." She lost herself in a kind of memory from which she emerged to affirm, smiling, "We cannot be separated, whether I speak or not."

Loving in him, perhaps—although she resented him for it— this overly strong tendency to fade away when faced with that which she could not say to him.

❖ "We have not yet begun to wait, have we?" — "What do you mean?" — "That if we could proceed in such a way that waiting begins, we could also be finished with it." — "But do we want to be finished with it all that much?" — "Yes, we want that; we want only that."

"Everything would change if we waited together." — "If the waiting were common to us? If we belonged to it in common? But isn't that what we are waiting for, to be together?" — "Yes, together." — "But in waiting." — "Together, waiting and without waiting."

❖ He wonders if solitude could be related to her presence, not directly but because she would oblige him—not that he would ever be able to succeed completely in this—to live in an impersonal manner. When he touched her and drew her toward himself in a movement to which she immediately consented, he knew, however, that their two images remained at a certain distance from each other, a slight distance that he did not lose the hope of reducing a little further.

❖ The bed is parallel to the table and to the wall opened by two windows. It is a couch wide enough for them to lie next to each other. She is nestled against the wall, turned toward the one who is firmly holding her.

❖ He knows that there is a certain coincidence between the place and the attention. It is a place of attention. The attention will never be directed at him, were he to remain there eternally. But he does not desire to be the object of this attention, either.

There is a certain, cold happiness in remaining, unknown, in the company of an extreme impersonal attention.

The attention is ignorant of everything about him; he senses it only through the infinite negligence in which it keeps him, but, with extreme delicacy and by means of constant imperceptible contacts, it has always already detached him from himself and makes him free for the attention that for an instant he becomes.

❖ The mystery is nothing, even as a mysterious nothing. It cannot be the object of attention. The mystery is the center of attention when attention, being equal and at perfect equality with itself, is the absence of any center.

In attention, the center of attention disappears, the central point around which perspective, sight, and the order of that which is to be seen inwardly and outwardly are distributed.

Attention is idle and uninhabited. Empty, it is the clarity of the emptiness.

Mystery: its essence is to be always on this side of attention. And the essence of attention is the ability to preserve, in and through itself, that which is always on this side of attention and the source of all waiting: mystery.

Attention, the welcoming of that which escapes attention, an opening onto the unexpected, waiting that is the unexpected in all waiting.

❖ She began a short time later: "I would like to speak to you."

From then on she had not stopped conversing with him, but nothing had struck him so much as the first words.

She proved, with respect to herself, to be so astonishingly indiscreet that her only purpose—of this he had no doubt— was to confine him to a discretion that was almost incompatible with life.

"You listen to the story as if it concerned something moving, remarkable, interesting." He does listen in this way.

A story that requires only a little attention. But also the waiting that gives attention.

❖ Someone in me converses with himself.

Someone in me converses with someone. I do not hear them. However, without me to separate them and without this separation that I maintain between them, they would not hear each other.

❖ He realized that she was attracted by light, but by a particular light whose source seemed to be some point of the description that he had tacitly accepted never to stop maintaining.

Do not describe that as if you remembered it.

❖ When he asks himself, "What does she expect of me?" he suspects that she has no expectations but rather is at the limit of expectation.

❖ She did not wait, he did not wait. Between them, however, the waiting.

❖ The attention waits. He does not know if this attention is his, separated from him and waiting outside him. He remains only with it.

The attention that waiting gathers in him is destined not to arrive at the accomplishment of that which he awaits, but rather to let all accomplishable things diverge through waiting alone, the approach of the unaccomplishable.

Only waiting gives attention. Empty time, with no project, is waiting that gives attention.

Through attention, he was not attentive to himself, or to anything that was related to anything else, but rather was carried, by the endlessness of waiting, to the extreme limit that escapes waiting.

Waiting gives attention while withdrawing everything that is awaited.

Through attention, he has at his disposal the endlessness of waiting. This endlessness exposes him to that which cannot be awaited, while carrying him to the extreme limit that does not allow itself to be reached.

❖ There was no longer any danger other than the danger of words without attention.

Attention never left him; in it he was cruelly abandoned.

❖ He did not think that one utterance had more importance than another; each one was more important than all the others; each sentence was the fundamental sentence, yet they attempted only to gather all together in the single one among them that need not have been proffered.

❖ "Never will you give a response to such an utterance." Immediately, he straightens up and asks, "Who said that?" And as a great silence reigns everywhere, he asks again, "Who is keeping the silence?"

He is well aware that she speaks and that there is no one to return the silence to her, no one to receive it from her.

❖ It seemed to him—he had been observing her so closely for so long—that she was drawing imperceptibly away and was attracting him in her movement of withdrawal. They were both withdrawing, immobile, leaving room for their immobility. Lying next to each other, tightly holding each other, and when she moves away, she is recaptured; at a remove, enveloping him again; at a distance without distance, touching her not touching him.

❖ The uncharted space of dread.

❖ When, upon awakening, he recognized the room where he had spent the night, he was pleased with his choice. It was a room in a modest hotel, the kind he liked, fairly narrow but long, abnormally long. Beside him, the body of the young woman facing the other way. He remembered that she had spoken to him late into the night.

❖ He said to her, and she appeared to be struck by these words, "I have not known him any longer than you have." Later, she tried to refute this statement: "But," she said, "it is only since I have known you that you do not know him."

"What would happen if my speech were suddenly to make itself heard by me?"

"In order to hear me, it would not be necessary to hear me, but rather to give me to be heard."

❖ Since when had he been waiting? Waiting is always a wait for waiting, wherein the beginning is withheld, the end suspended, and the interval of another wait thus opened. The night in which nothing is awaited represents this moment of waiting.

The impossibility of waiting belongs essentially to waiting.

He realized that he had written only so that he could respond to the impossibility of waiting. What was said, therefore, was related to waiting. This illumination flashed through him, but did nothing more than that.

❖ Since when had he started to wait? Since he had made himself free for waiting by losing the desire for particular things, including the desire for the end of things. Waiting begins when there is nothing more to wait for, not even the end of waiting. Waiting is unaware of and destroys that which it awaits. Waiting awaits nothing.

Whatever the importance of the object of waiting may be, it is always infinitely surpassed by the movement of waiting. Waiting renders all things equally important, equally vain. In order to wait for the slightest thing, we have at our disposal an infinite capacity for waiting that seems inexhaustible.

"Waiting does not console." — "Those who wait have nothing to be consoled about."

❖ Even if waiting is related to the anxiety that he experiences, waiting, with its own tranquil anxiety, dissolved his a long time ago. He feels liberated by waiting for waiting.

❖ They are already such ancient utterances and, when she formulates them, thought for such a long time that they represent a truth that is brilliant outside, extinguished inside.

Everything she says represents ancient thoughts and previous utterances. Elsewhere, he would understand them; in this place, he hears them too late.

❖ Enveloped in herself, turned toward and away from him; how could he see her? He must struggle against a thought that, as soon as he looks at it, looks at him.

❖ "Don't talk about that. Don't think about that any longer; forget everything." — "I have forgotten everything. I have also forgotten you."* — "Yes, you have forgotten me."

There is no real dialogue between them. Only waiting maintains between what they say a certain relation, words spoken to wait, a waiting of words.

❖ In waiting, each word become slow and solitary.

*The female interlocutor says this.

❖ He was supposed to precede her and to take the lead always, without any assurances of ever being followed by her. He was obliged first to discover the words with which she could then make him hear what she had to say to him. They proceeded in this way, motionless within movement.

❖ Always the same morning light.

❖ When he looked at her too long, he sees in her place and superimposed on her a kind of absence of a person that he does not dread having to look at further.

❖ Sterile waiting, always poorer and emptier. Full waiting, always richer in waiting. The one is the other.

❖ The thought that she is there, although through her words she always denies her presence in a certain way while affirming its secret relation to herself.

❖ The countless population of emptiness.

❖ The same day was going by.

❖ He had seen her once, twice, an infinite number of times. He had passed close to her and had not effaced her presence. He had never doubted that she knew nothing about him. She was ignorant of him; he accepted her ignorance. At first, what energy, what a profound life because of this redoubled solitude; at the end, what heaviness of deception and error. Whoever has accepted that once must persevere without end.

She is ignorant of him, even as she is more attentive than anyone else to what he does and says.

It seems to him that she does not doubt her presence any more than she invests it with faith. Perhaps because she does not doubt, she does not believe.

❖ She had placed all her faith in this thing in which she did not believe.

❖ She is not attentive to what he does: he does nothing, nor any more so to what he says: he speaks less than he listens; to himself, perhaps, to this him that waiting disengages from him and that is the attentive indifference of the place.

It was the heartbeats, the restlessness of hope, the anxiety of illusion.

❖ He had endured waiting. Waiting made him eternal, and now he has nothing more to do than to wait eternally.

Waiting waits. Through waiting, he who waits dies waiting. He maintains waiting in death and seems to make of death the waiting for that which is still awaited when one dies.

Death, considered as an event that one awaits, is incapable of putting an end to waiting. Waiting transforms the fact of dying into something that one does not merely have to attain in order to cease waiting. Waiting is what allows us to know that death cannot be awaited.

He who lives in a state of waiting sees life come to him as the emptiness of waiting and waiting as the emptiness of the beyond of life. The unstable indeterminateness of these two movements is henceforth the space of waiting. At every step, one is here, and yet beyond. But as this beyond is reached without being reached through death, it is awaited and is not reached; without knowing that its essential characteristic is to be able to be reached only in waiting.*

When there is waiting, nothing is awaited. In the movement of waiting, death ceases to be able to be awaited. Waiting, in the intimate tranquillity at the heart of which everything that comes

*This passage announces Blanchot's next fragmentary work, *Le Pas au-delà*.

to pass is diverted by waiting, does not let death come to pass as that which could be adequate to waiting but rather keeps it in suspense, in dissolution, and at every instant surpassed by the empty sameness of waiting.

The strange opposition of waiting and death. He waits for death, in a state of waiting indifferent to death. And, similarly, death does not let itself be awaited.

❖ The dead came back to life dying.

❖ "You respond with my questions." — "I make of your questions a response."

❖ When she began to look for expressions to say to him, "You will never know. You will never make me speak. Never will you learn why I am here with you," it was then, in the vehement movement that allowed her to be an impassioned voice while remaining a motionless and impassive body, that he heard her suddenly ask him, without even changing the register of her voice and perhaps even without changing her words: "Act in such a way that I can speak to you." He would never again be able to forget this request.

For days he had struggled against her, through words, through silences: "No, I am not the one you would like me to be." About which, much later, she interjected, "And who would you be if you were?" Since he did not want to give a specific reply, because of a kind of reservation or perhaps some more serious difficulty, she concluded triumphantly, "You see, you cannot say it, let alone deny it."

❖ "You do not speak toward me; you speak toward someone who is not here to hear you." — "But you are here?" — "I am here."

❖ He never dreamed about her. She never dreamed about him.

They were both dreamed only by the one they would have liked to be for each other.

❖ She was lying down, partially facing the other way. The table against the bed, he writes with a continuous noise that makes the silence almost transparent. All of a sudden, she addresses him with this question: "Who are you really? You cannot be you, but you are someone. Who?" He interrupted his work, lowers his head. "I am questioning you." He, too, is questioning himself. "Do not have any doubts," he says softly. "I choose to be that which finds me. I am indeed what you just said." — "Who?" She is almost shouting. "Yes, what you just said."

❖ The two of us together, we know.

❖ The decaying of waiting, boredom. Stagnant waiting, waiting that at first took itself as its object, complacent with itself and finally hateful of itself. Waiting, the calm anguish of waiting; waiting become the calm expanse where thought is present in waiting.

❖ She was seated, motionless, at the table, lying next to him on the bed, sometimes standing next to the door and then coming from very far away. This is how he had seen her the first time. Standing, having entered without saying a word and not even looking around, as if she had always gathered in herself all the presence of the place; and assuredly if there had not been between him and every feminine figure a long familiarity that made him close to each of them, he would necessarily have felt like an intruder in this room, but with the firm assurance of youth, he saw nothing more extraordinary in her coming than he did in the fact that he had not hesitated to make a sign to her a short while ago: she was here; he would not let her leave. He was here; she would not let him leave.

❖ "When you recall that I abandoned you, it is true. When you say with sadness that I did not even abandon you, it is true. But when you think that I was abandoned by myself, who, then, is now next to you?"*

❖ "Come." She approached slowly, not in spite of herself but with a kind of profound distraction that made him wondrously attentive.

She had spoken, but he did not listen to her. He listened to her only so that he could attract her to him by his attention.

❖ Narrow the presence, vast the place.

❖ "Ah, finally, you say it candidly." — "Why? Haven't I always been candid?" — "Very candid, too candid, perhaps, for the truth without candor that is attempting to express itself through you."

He knew that there was nothing else either in her or in him than the effort to reach this thought that, outside them, waited for them to show them the way or to lead them astray.

If he had forced her to speak, never had he exerted any pressure on her so that he could enter her thought. He did not attribute any thoughts to her. The word *thought* did not contain enough transparency, enough obscurity. She only spoke, she only kept silent.

❖ He attracted her; how had he attracted her? He attracted her constantly, by an immobile, imperceptible force. She was the very place of this attraction that he exerted over her and that she exerted over him through the return of attraction: arrested here and not immovable, immobile, of a wandering immobility.

A vagabond outside herself all the way to him outside himself.

❖ What had she forgotten? Was it very important? Oh, no, it was insignificant. She said that with a kind of furious peace, a tranquillity bathed in tears, traversed by light, heavy with obscurity.

*The male interlocutor is speaking here.

❖ "Why do you think that?" — "I think it, I always will. It is a thought that one cannot put an end to." He shuddered upon hearing this kind of condemnation.

❖ "Do you think that they remember?" — "No, they forget." — "Do you think that forgetting is the manner in which they remember?" — "No, they forget and retain nothing in forgetting." — "Do you think that what is lost in forgetting is preserved in forgetting from forgetting?" — "No, forgetting is indifferent to forgetting." — "So, we will be wondrously, profoundly, eternally forgotten?" — "Forgotten without wonder, without profundity, without eternity."

❖ Together they went into the room, slowly, lightly, adeptly moving around each obstacle, looking for an instant out the window: together, not knowing it, speaking to each other, responding to each other in vain; continuing all the same to speak for each other calmly and gently.

❖ (Two beings from here, two ancient gods. They were in my room; I lived with them.

For an instant, I joined in their dialogue. They were not surprised. "Who are you? One of the new gods?" — "No, no, just a man." But my denial did not stop them. "Ah, the new gods! They have finally come."

Their curiosity was light, capricious, wondrous. "What are you doing here?" I answered them. They did not listen to me. They knew everything; theirs was a light knowledge that could not be weighed down with the kind of partial truth that I gave to them.

They were beautiful, but the attention that I paid to her had the effect of making her almost constantly alone for me, thanks to which her beauty became even more striking. I could tell that I attracted her as well, in spite of the fact that she seemed to be ignorant of me, of me in particular. She appeared to me in a real

31

way; she was a tall girl whom I was amazed to be able to look at, although I was not capable of describing her, and when I said to her, "Come," she immediately drew nearer with a profound distraction that made me extremely attentive. He then disappeared for good. At least, it was more practical for me to think that he did. Does a god disappear?

We have been living together ever since. And I almost no longer resist the idea that one day I may be the new god.)

The dream of a dreamless night.

❖ She desired forgetting extraordinarily: "Are we in forgetting here?" — "Not yet." — "Why is that?" — "We are waiting." — "Yes, we are waiting."

Forgetting, waiting. Waiting that assembles, disperses; forgetting that disperses, assembles. Waiting, forgetting. "Will you forget me?" — "Yes, I will." — "How will you be sure that you have forgotten me?" — "I will be sure when I remember another woman." — "But I am still the one you will remember; I need more." — "You will have more: I will be sure when I no longer remember myself." She reflected on this idea, which appeared to please her. "Forgotten together. And who, then, will forget us? Who will be sure of us in forgetting?" — "The others, all the others!" — "But they don't count. I couldn't care less about being forgotten by the others. I want to be forgotten by you and you alone." — "Well, then, I will be sure when you have forgotten me." — "But," she said sadly, "I have a feeling that I have forgotten you already."

She forgot him; she recalled all things, but she forgot him in everything: slowly, passionately. When she had come in—Had he made a sign to her? Had he made use of this effortlessness of attraction?—she was already in this movement of forgetting that attempted to say everything so that everything would be forgotten, entrusting the imperishable to the ephemeral individual.

She forgot, she was almost forgetting and the visible beauty of that which was forgotten.

❖ Only the gods reach forgetting: the ancient ones so as to move farther away, the new ones so as to return.

❖ She did not forget him; she forgot. He was still for her, in the forgetting where he had disappeared in her, everything that he was. And he forgot her, too: one cannot remember someone who does not remember.
However, everything remained unchanged.

❖ Of this, he was well aware: he pushed her gently toward forgetting. Attracting her toward him, he attracted her toward someone she always forgot more profoundly, more superficially. The words had been said, the utterances burned, the silence traversed by fire. They were still pressed against each other, both of them deprived of themselves. "Why must I forget you?" Was forgetting the ultimate goal? Waiting, forgetting.

"I have known you only so that I can know nothing of you and lose myself completely in you."

❖ Don't gods live in this way? Solitary, unique, unfamiliar with the light that emanates from them. They hardly disturbed me, it is true. I had grown accustomed to their presence. I rejoiced in being unknown to them, but I was unable to determine if this ignorance was a result of their extreme discretion or a divine indifference. The ancient gods, the ancient gods, how near they are to us.

❖ Forgetting, the acquiescence to forgetting in the remembrance that forgets nothing.

❖ "It is you who pushed me into forgetting."* — "Gently, you must admit." — "Yes, gently, tenderly; nothing was more gentle."

*The female character leads off in this fragment.

33

— "It was the gentleness of forgetting in its attraction." — "And why, then, did you make me remember?" — "To make you forget." — "But I had necessarily forgotten everything." — "Not in accordance with the necessity of forgetting."

He waits, she forgets, in an identical movement that could bring them back to each other. But waiting, he knows, forbids him this meeting, which could take place only in the present instant. Waiting is instancy always without the present instant.

"You made me speak; why? Why all these words that you gave to me?" — "I received rather than gave them." — "They came to me from your waiting, as you well know, and in them I believe that I have forgotten everything." — "Forgetting is also a good thing." — "Yes, you wish, through these words of forgetting, to make me ever more absent." — "That is, forgetting is still your presence in each word."

❖ You will never find the limits of forgetting, no matter how far you may be able to forget.

❖ "But if I remembered everything and told you everything, there would be nothing more for us than a single memory." — "A common memory? No," he said solemnly, "we shall never belong in common to memory." — "To forgetting, then." — "Perhaps to forgetting." — "Yes, when I forget, I already feel closer to you." — "In a proximity, however, without approach." — "That is correct," she echoed fervently, "without approach." — "Also without truth, without secrecy." — "Without truth, without secrecy." — "As if disappearance were the last place of any meeting. Forgetting will separate us slowly, patiently, through an identically unknown movement, from whatever still remains in common between us." She reflected while listening to him, then resumed in a lower voice, "Provided that forgetting remains in an utterance." — "An utterance of forgetting." — "Will everything, then, be forgotten in an instant?" — "Each thing in all things." — "And how will the instant in which everything is forgotten be forgotten?" — "Forgetting descends into forgetting."

❖ To wait was to wait for the opportunity. And the opportunity came only at the instant stolen from waiting, the instant when it is no longer a question of waiting.

❖ Being is yet another word for forgetting.

❖ "Didn't I always tell you everything?" — "Yes, it is true, you were wonderful." He stopped. "But that may have been our misfortune." And, as she said nothing: "It was our misfortune. From the first instant, you spoke intimately, wonderfully to me. I will never forget those first instants when everything was already said between us. But I failed not to know. I have never been able to learn anything except what I knew." — "I had confidence in you; I spoke to you as if I were speaking to myself." — "Yes, but you knew; I did not." — "Why didn't you warn me? You should have interrupted me." — "The effect was too strong; I desired nothing more, I could have nothing more." She reflected on this, and all of a sudden, as if her mind were made up, she turned toward him with strange solemnity: "Did I really speak to you from the first instant as I would have to someone to whom I would have already said everything, everything that I wanted to say?" — "Yes, I believe so; that is correct." — "Well, therein was the secret: I had already told you everything." And, since he did not respond, "You are disappointed. You were waiting for something else." — "No, no," he said, shaking his head. "It was wonderful."

❖ He knew what his first word had been; he was certain that by saying to her: "Come"—and she had immediately drawn near—he had made her enter this circle of attraction where one could begin to speak only because everything had already been said. Was he too close to her? Was there no longer enough distance between them? And wasn't she too familiar in her strangeness?

He had attracted her; that was his magic, his mistake. "You did not attract me; you haven't attracted me yet."

❖ The more she forgot him, the more she felt attracted by waiting toward the place that she was occupying with him.

"Why are you so interested in this room?" — "Am I interested in it?" — "Let's just say that it attracts you." — "Actually, you attracted me to it."

He had called her; she had come. Coming from his call, calling him in her coming.

"What you say may have too much meaning, an exclusive meaning. As if it could not be expressed anywhere else but here." — "Isn't that what is necessary?" — "I do not simply mean that in another place everything would have another meaning, but rather that there is something in your words that speaks constantly of this place where we are. Why? What, then, is happening here? It must be said." — "It is up to you to know that, since it is already said in my words that you are alone in hearing."

Alone in hearing. That necessitates on his part a severity of attention that does not content itself with perseverance.

"What is happening here? For the moment, we are speaking." — "Yes, we are speaking." — "But we did not come here to speak." — "All the same, we came speaking."

❖ She was there, it is true. He kept her completely under his gaze, gathered in herself, distracted from her in herself. And he saw her constantly, flawlessly, and yet as if by accident. She had no other face than this wondrous, troubling certainty.

Visible, but not seen on account of this visibility.

Not visible and not invisible, affirming her right to be seen by him by virtue of a light that always preceded light; and perhaps it was not a true light, but only a clarity that together they shared, which had come from the secret of themselves and was restored to the ignorance of themselves. A clarity without clarity, a distant affirmation of the attraction, a melancholy and happy knowledge resulting from the fact that he was not looking at her yet. The face, the highest affirmation of her right to be seen by him, even if she had not been visible.

❖ "Do you see me?" — "Of course, I see you; I see only you— but not yet."

❖ What you have written holds the secret. She no longer has it; she gave it to you, and it is only because it escaped you that you were able to transcribe it.

❖ The language of attraction, heavy, obscure language, saying everything where everything is said, language of shuddering and of space without spacing. She had told him everything because he had attracted her and she had attached herself to him. But attraction is the attraction toward the place where, as soon as one enters, everything is said.

❖ "Do you see me?" — "Naturally, I see you." — "That is precious little; everyone can see me." — "But perhaps not as I see you." — "I would like something else; I want something else. It is very important. Would you know how to see me even if you were unable to see me?" — "If you were invisible?" He thought: "Undoubtedly: inside myself." — "I do not mean: truly invisible; I do not ask for so much. But I would not want you to see me for the simple reason that I am visible." — "May no one other than I see you!" — "No, no, I don't care if I am visible for everyone, but I would like to be seen by you alone for a more serious reason, you understand, and . . ." — "A more certain one?" — "More certain, but not really certain; without the guarantee that makes visible things visible." — "Always, then?" — "Always, always, but not yet."

It seemed to him that he took possession of this dialogue in the very sight that he had of her, like a warning that he would understand only later.

If we are visible by virtue of a power that precedes us, then he saw her outside this power, by virtue of a right without light that evoked the idea of a transgression, an extraordinary transgression.

❖ The face, the extreme and cruel limit where that which is going to make her extremely visible is diffused in the calm clarity that comes from her.

❖ She speaks to him; he does not hear her. And yet it is in him that she makes herself heard by me.

I know nothing of him; I make no room for him inside or outside myself. But if she speaks to him, I hear her in he who does not hear her.

❖ He remained so that she could be forgotten. He watched over the forgetting where she was leading him, by a calm movement that came from forgetting. Forgetting, forgotten. "If I forget you, will you remember yourself?" — "Myself, in your forgetting of me." — "But is it I who shall forget you; is it you who will remember?" — "Not you, not I: the forgetting will forget me in you, and the impersonal remembrance will efface me from that which remembers." — "If I forget you, will the forgetting then eternally attract you outside yourself?" — "Eternally outside myself in the attraction of forgetting." — "Is this what we are together from this moment on?" — "This is what we are from this moment on, but not yet." — "Together?" — "Together, but not yet."

❖ She speaks to him; he does not hear her; I hear her in him.

❖ The one who, forgetting, is effaced from us in this forgetting also effaces in us the personal ability to remember; then the impersonal remembrance is awakened, the personless remembrance that takes the place of forgetting for us.

❖ In her he remembered the day, the night, that which had lasted, that which had finished lasting, but he did not remember herself in her.

He would forget, if he remembered.

He did not know if now he was forgetting the words or if the words were gently and obscurely forgetting.

The clear forgetting, the gentle remembrance of words, to go in them from remembrance to forgetting. In their transparency or, for lack thereof, in their abstract poverty, he recognized the submissive luminosity of forgetting. The submissive appearance of forgetting in them, submission that calls for the greatest submission.

We would forget, if we could be submissive to the forgetting that the words made for forgetting dispense to us at every instant, and at least once.

❖ A hurried, eternal step.

They complain about eternity; it is as if eternity were complaining in them. "What more do you want?" They still bear the strange desire to die that they were unable to satisfy in dying.

Forgetting, nothing except forgetting, the image of forgetting, the image returned, by waiting, to forgetting.

"And now, are we forgotten?" — "If you can say 'we,' we are forgotten." — "Not yet, I beg of you, not yet." The silent walking, the mute, closed space where desire wanders endlessly.

He walked ahead, marking out for her a path toward himself, and she held onto him tightly, in a movement in which they were commingled, walking in his steps at the same pace, only hurried, eternal.

"You will still have other companions." — "Perhaps, but a woman other than myself will accompany them." — "Another woman, and yet no one else." — "Another man and no other."

He lives in the imminence of a thought that is only the thought of eternal imminence.

❖ When she had asked of him, a stranger, what someone close to her would not have been close enough to give her, he understood that in asking it of him, she had made him closer than any other. Why had he instantly accepted such closeness?

"Do you still want me to do it?" — "In asking you to do it, I also entrusted you with this wish."

He had refused, but what he had refused was still before him, unknown to his consent so as to be unknown to his refusal.

"When did you have this idea?" — "When I knew that I had it, it had been familiar to me for a long time." — "Actually, you must never have thought that; when you thought about it, it was only so that you could refuse to think it." — "But the refusal was part of the thought."

He had understood that what was asked of him did not stop at the simple act that could have appeared to be adequate to the request, especially when she had suggested to him, with provocative gentleness: "And yet, isn't it easy?" — "Easy, perhaps, but not practicable." To which she had found this response a short time later: "That is, it can be done only once."

❖ "What you ask of me . . ." — "I do not ask it of you." — "That changes nothing: you would like to have asked it of me." — "I do not believe that I can want that; perhaps I have never wanted it." — "Is it, then, more vast than any wanting? Didn't you want it in any way?" — "I was only afraid of it; I was afraid to want it."

❖ What is she asking for? Why doesn't this request reach him?

"It is as if you were asking for that which would prevent you from asking for it. Therefore, you do not ask for it." — "I do not ask for it; I place it in your hand."

At once, what an impression: his hand closing around the truth, this hand that, far from him, opens her eyes.

❖ She asked for nothing; she merely said something that he could sustain only in relation to this request.

She asked for nothing; she only asked. A request that she had had to present to him from the first instants and that since then— at least he had convinced himself of this—had been erratically marking out a path toward him through everything she said.

❖ What he thought was turned away from his thought so as to let him purely think this detour.

❖ What was asked of him and could not be asked; that which, once accomplished, would still remain to be accomplished: he lived and thought about the meeting point of these two movements that were not in opposition to each other, but rather that questioned each other two by two.

"Give that to me." As if in asking that of him, she had waited for the plenitude of the only gift that he could not give her.

❖ The calm detour of thought, the return from itself to itself in waiting.

Through waiting, what is turned away from thought returns to thought, having become its detour.

Waiting, the space of the detour without digression, of wandering without error.

❖ "Why do you ask that of me?" — "You are the person I need: I have always known it." — "And where did you get this idea?" She did not think for very long: "From you, as you well know. You attracted me through this idea." — "Do you want to admit that far from knowing anything about it, I could not express it?" — "This proves that it is already in you more profoundly than it is in me." — "No, believe me, I do not know it." — "Together we both know it."

He sensed that this thought was not actually common to them, but rather that they would be in common only in this thought.

❖ That which escapes without anything being hidden.

❖ "You asked it of me because it is impossible." — "Impossible, but possible if I was able to ask it of you." — "Everything, then, depends on whether you really asked it of me?" — "Everything depends on that."

❖ "Suppose that you asked of me what you did because I would have already done it." — "But you would know." — "No more than you would. This is how things may have transpired: you asked it of me, I did it, but neither of us knows the relation of these two decisions; I mean that the only thing we know about them is the familiar relation that still hides them from both of us and makes them for us even now unfulfillable and inaccessible. How could I have done something that, without your asking, I would have been unable even to anticipate? But how could you ask such a thing of me if you had not already learned and comprehended it through its accomplishment in yourself?"

❖ "Each time you refuse, you refuse the inevitable." — "The impossible." — "You make the impossible inevitable."

❖ That which escapes without anything being hidden, which is affirmed but remains unexpressed, which is here and forgotten. Thought accomplished itself unsuspected in this surprise: that she was always and each time a presence.

❖ She was present, already her own image, and her image, not the remembrance, the forgetting of herself. When seeing her, he saw her as she would be, forgotten.

Sometimes he forgot her, sometimes he remembered, sometimes remembering the forgetting and forgetting everything in this remembrance.

"Perhaps we are separated only by our presence. In forgetting, what will separate us?" — "Yes, what could separate us?" —

"Nothing, except the forgetting that will reunite us." — "But what if it is really forgetting?"

Was it possible that she recognized in him, and he in her, a capacity to be forgotten commensurate with waiting?

❖ "We did not meet." — "Let's say that we crossed paths: that is even better." — "How painful it is, this encounter with the crossing."

❖ For a long time, he had been trying not to say anything that would encumber space, speaking space, exhausting finite and limitless space.

❖ "I always felt that you didn't really want to know." He did not. One knows nothing when one wants to know.

❖ No one likes to remain face to face with that which is hidden. "Face to face would be easy, but not in an oblique relation."

❖ "All those gazes from you that did not look at me." — "All those words that you said and that did not speak to me." — "And your presence that lingers and resists." — "And you already absent."

Where was it? Where was it not?

Knowing that she was here, and having forgotten her so perfectly, knowing that she could be here only by being forgotten, and knowing it, forgetting it himself.

"Is there still an instant?" — "The instant that is between remembering and forgetting." — "A brief instant." — "Which does not cease." — "As for us, neither remembered nor forgotten." — "Remembering through forgetting."

"Why this happiness in forgetting?" — "Happiness itself forgotten."

It is death, she said, the forgetting to die that is death. The future finally present. "Act in such a way that I can speak to you."

— "Yes, speak to me now." — "I cannot." — "Speak without the ability to do so." — "You ask me so calmly to do the impossible."

What is this pain, this fear, what is this light? The forgetting of light in light.

II

Forgetting, the latent gift.*

To welcome forgetting as the accord with that which is hidden, the latent gift.

We do not go toward forgetting any more than forgetting comes to us, but suddenly forgetting has always already been here, and when we forget, we have always already forgotten everything: we are, in the movement toward forgetting, in relation with the presence of the immobility of forgetting.

Forgetting is a relation with that which is forgotten, a relation that, making secret that with which there is a relation, possesses the power and meaning of the secret.

In forgetting, there is that which turns away, and there is this detour that comes from forgetting, which is forgetting.

❖ Later on, he awakened calmly, cautiously, facing the possibility that he had already forgotten everything.

*Note the phonetic resemblance in French between the adjective *latent* and *l'attente*. Blanchot returns to this play on words on two occasions, on page 73 and in the final sentence of the text. Here, *le don latent* (the latent gift) can also be read as *le don l'attend* (the gift awaits him or her).

Forgetting a word, forgetting in this word all words.

❖ "Come, and give back to us the propriety of that which disappears, the movement of a heart."

❖ It was strange that forgetting could rely in this way on speech and that speech could welcome forgetting, as if there were a relation between the detour of speech and the detour of forgetting.

Writing in the direction of forgetting.

That forgetting speaks in advance in every word that speaks does not only signify that each word is destined to be forgotten, but also that forgetting finds its repose in speech and keeps speech in accord with that which is hidden.

Forgetting, in the repose that all true speech accords it, lets her speak even in forgetting.

May forgetting repose in all speech.

❖ "You will not enter this place twice." — "I will enter it, but not even once."

Keeping watch over that which is not watched over.

❖ Through her words, he learned in what a calm way forgetting relies on speech.

The memory where forgetting breathed.

The breath that he receives from her, which traverses the entire story, the breathing of forgetting.

❖ In forgetting, that which turns away cannot completely hide the detour that comes from forgetting.

"Could it be that to forget death is actually to remember it? Would forgetting be the only remembrance commensurate with death?" — "Impossible forgetting. Each time you forget, it is death that you recall in forgetting."

Forgetting death, meeting the point where death sustains forgetting and forgetting gives death, turning away from death through forgetting and from forgetting through death, thus turning away twice to enter the truth of the detour.

The initiative of forgetting in motionless waiting.

❖ Keeping watch over the unwatched presence.

Look at her for an instant, over your shoulder; look toward her with a half-look; do not look at her, look; look only with a half-look.

She was almost too present; not present: exposed to her presence; not absent, either: separated from present things by the strength of her presence in her.

❖ "And why, then, would I continue?" — "I know why: so that you can affirm to yourself with certainty that you will not speak." — "Then show some consideration for that which I am unable to say to you."

What she said—he did not fail to warn her of this—did not stop struggling valiantly, obscurely. "Against what?" — "Our ability to discover that is also without a doubt the price of this struggle." — "But against what?" — "You must continue to struggle to know that." — "Well, then, I do know: against this presence." — "What presence?" — "Mine, the one that responded to your call." And as he said nothing, "What about you? Are you struggling with me?" — "I am struggling with you, but only so that you will accept your presence as I have."

She would have liked, as he was well aware, to make him doubt her presence, at least if the word *doubt* had had as much strength and dignity as she seemed to attribute to it.

"I do not doubt you; I never will." — "I know, but what about my presence?" — "I doubt it even less." — "You see, you prefer it."

She was almost too present, of a presence that painfully exceeded her ability to let her always be present, there, motionless before him, even when she followed him, even when he held her tightly against himself, and when she spoke, speaking as if beside her presence; when she approached, approaching on account of her presence.

Coming in her presence.

When she approached, not making her presence any closer, approaching only in the space of her presence.

Her presence had no relation to what was present in her.

What he really had to consider as a fragment of strange light is the suspicion that she unceasingly cast on what she called her presence, affirming that he could not fail to entertain certain relations with her presence from which she was excluded. She spoke, the presence said nothing; she went away, the presence was there, not waiting, a stranger to waiting and never awaited. He had tried to convince her that he did not make any distinction between them; she shook her head: "I have my privileges, it has its privileges. Why does it have such a hold over you?" — "Because it makes you present." — "It does not make me present. Don't you sense that it is between us?" He reflected, almost painfully: "Is that what you wanted to say to me?" — "But it prevents me from saying it to you." — "You are saying it now." — "I haven't said it yet."*

❖ Wanting to and not being able to speak; not wanting to and not being able to evade speech; thus speaking–not speaking, in an identical movement that her interlocutor had the duty to maintain.

Speaking, not wanting to; wanting to, not being able to.

❖ "In that case, the same applies to me." — "No, it doesn't, as you well know." — "Why wouldn't you have relations with my presence that you refuse me, if I have such relations with your presence?" — "I do not refuse you anything." — "But is it possible that you speak to him?" She thought about this, and, with sudden fervor: "They

*Here and in a few subsequent fragments where the topic under consideration is "her presence," the pronoun *it* can also be read as *she* (since *elle* is used to refer to the feminine antecedent *présence*), which creates the impression that a second woman has entered the picture and has even come between the two interlocutors.

must be together, they are together; they keep us at a distance." He looked in her direction: "Well, then, we will get along without them; we have our compensations." — "Yes, we will get along without them, but," she added immediately, "will you be loyal?" — "I will," and as he thought about the consequences: "What must I do to be loyal?" But she repeated with firm assuredness: "You will be, you will conduct yourself honorably."

He knew in part what she might fear. However, when she said in a low voice, but so rapidly that it was as if he were drawn into what she wanted to say to him, "Don't leave me, don't; that would be worse than death," he had the impression of coming up against the truth of her torment for the very first time.

❖ "I can no longer bear my presence next to you."

❖ They waited, they sought each other out, turned away from their presence to be present to each other. She did not come to him only from the depths of waiting; how crude it would have been to think that. She was there through the abrupt decision of her presence, outside all waiting, and it was because she could not make herself wait, because she continually said secretly, manifestly, and with the impulsiveness of the simplest desire: "I cannot wait any longer," that he was the one who found himself exposed to the endlessness of waiting.

Reunited, waiting to be reunited.

❖ In waiting, time lost.

Waiting gives time, takes time, but it is not the same time that is given and that is taken. As if, waiting, he lacked only the time to wait.

This overabundance of time that is lacking, this overabundant lack of time.

"Is this going to last much longer?" — "Forever, if you experience it as a length of time."

Waiting does not leave him the time to wait.

❖ It was as if they had lost the idea that they could die. Whence came the desperate tranquillity, the unbearable daylight.

❖ When you affirm, you still question. The fact is that he must speak in waiting.

❖ Waiting imperceptibly changed the statements into questions. Searching in waiting for the question that waiting carries within itself. It is not a question that he can find and appropriate, nor is it even a proper manner of questioning. He says that he is searching; he is not searching, and if he questions, that is perhaps already unfaithful to waiting, which neither affirms nor questions, but waits.

The question that waiting carries within itself: it carries the question but does not become one with it. It is like a question that could be presented at the end of waiting, if the essence of waiting were not, even in coming to an end, to be unending.

The question of waiting: waiting carries a question that is not asked. Between the one and the other, there is in common infinity, which is in the slightest question as in the faintest waiting. As soon as someone questions, there is no response that would exhaust the question.

Attempting to reach through waiting, without releasing anything that questions and even less that responds, the measure appropriate to the essence of the response: not the measure that limits, but rather the measure that measures while reserving limitlessness.

❖ He was careful not to question her, waiting for a response that would answer no question.

"Am I really the one to whom you would like to speak?" — "Yes, I believe you are." — "But am I still the one, when you no longer want to speak to me?" — "That depends on you; you have to persevere."

He could not question her; did she understand that? Yes, she knew. It was like a prohibition: between them, something had already been said in advance that they had to take into account. "Always in me, and as if in front of me, something is there that casts its shadow on what I would like to say to you at the moment I say it to you."

Truth in their words would have been superfluous, which they had always admitted in tacit agreement.

He felt that the strength of his questions—the ones that he did not express but that he merely kept in reserve—was not to be drawn directly from his life; he felt as though he first had to exhaust his life through the movement of waiting and, with this presence without a present, make clear to her, and peaceful for her, what she avoided saying. But did she say it? Yes, that is how she forbade herself to say it. As if the same word would have expressed and yet impeded expression. Thus, it was up to him to separate without violence the superfluous things from the right things she said.

"If we were alive . . ." — "But we are alive!" — "You are, but you question me with something that is not alive in you and that seeks out something in me that cannot live any longer. That is cause for suffering, that is anguish."

❖ The movement of waiting: he saw her as if she were turned away from him by waiting, unless, turning back to see her, he had to turn away from himself, no longer seeing her except in this detour.

❖ Waiting is when time is always in excess and when time is nevertheless short on time. This overabundant lack of time is the duration of waiting.

In waiting, the time that allows him to wait is lost so that it can better respond to waiting.

Waiting that takes place in time opens time to the absence of time, where there is no reason to wait.

The absence of time is what lets him wait.

Time is what gives him something to wait for.

In waiting the absence of time reigns, where waiting is the impossibility of waiting.

Time makes impossible waiting, where the pressure of the absence of time is affirmed, possible.

In time, waiting comes to an end without being put to an end.

He knows that when time comes to an end, the absence of time is also dispersed or escapes. But, in waiting, if time always gives him something to wait for, whether it is his own end or the end of things, he is always destined for the absence of time, which has always released waiting from this end and every end.

❖ Waiting fulfilled by waiting, fulfilled/disappointed by waiting.

❖ "This presence." — "Your presence? Mine?" — "It is not so easy to tell them apart, as you know. My presence is very strong for you; it interests and holds your attention only too much. As for me, however, it is because I almost do not sense your presence any longer that it appears to me so powerful and almost invincible in its disappearance."

He had always suspected it: if he waited, it is because he was not alone, removed from his solitude so as to be dispersed in the solitude of waiting. Always alone to wait and always separated from himself by waiting that did not leave him alone.

The infinite dispersion of waiting always gathered together anew by the imminence of the end of waiting.

❖ If each thought is an allusion to the impossibility of thinking, if each time she adjourns thought so that she can think . . .

In waiting, he could ask no questions about waiting. What was he waiting for, why was he waiting, what is there to await in waiting? The essence of waiting is to escape all the forms of questioning that it makes possible and from which it is excluded.

Through waiting, each affirmation opened onto a void, and

each question was accompanied by another, more silent double that he could have caught by surprise.

The thought of waiting: thought that is the waiting for that which does not let itself be thought, thought borne by waiting that is adjourned in this waiting.

❖ "I can no longer endure my presence next to you." — "It is not next to me; it would not accept this manner of being next to someone." — "And yet it is here." It was there.

He tried to tell her that she must not let herself be held back by this thought. It was best to turn away from it without granting it any importance. That would be easy. It did not ask for any attention. "You must not think about it, either." — "No, I must not, and even if I were to think about it, I would not think about it." — "But you see it, you see it all the time." — "I do not see it, and only when you are here." — "I am here all the time." — "When you are here, it is not exactly time any more." — "If you do not see it, it must be seen." — "Is that what you desire?" — "It is the only thing I desire. I want you to look at it once and for all." — "Why?" — "So that you will see how different it is from me." — "But I will see only you in it.

"Would you go so far as to reject your presence?" And, as she did not answer: "And if I, too, were to reject it, wouldn't you feel affected? You cannot make any distinctions between you and your presence." — "Except the ones that you make yourself." — "I don't make any. Those that I do make do not tend to set you apart from your presence." — "We are not different, I can feel that. It is this indifference that it makes visible in a manner that I cannot bear."

Indifference clarifying presence.

"It is through this indifference that it attracts you." — "But does it attract me?" — "You attract it, you are both in the zone of attraction."

This presence of indifference in her, its attraction.

❖ Waiting and forgetting, ignorance and thought affirmed that which did not let itself be awaited in waiting, that which did not let itself be forgotten in forgetting, that of which ignorance was not ignorant, that which was unthought in thought.

The present that forgetting would make for them: presence free of any present, with no relation to being, turned away from every possibility and impossibility.

❖ She forgot more slowly than any slowness, more suddenly than any surprise.

"I sometimes have the impression that you remember only so that you can forget: so that you can keep the power of forgetting perceptible. It is rather forgetting that you would like to remember." — "Perhaps. I remember when I am two steps away from forgetting. It is a strange impression." — "A dangerous one as well; the distance of two steps can be quickly covered." — "Yes, but there will always be two more steps, and each time I sense that you are following me, you who are nevertheless in front of me." — "I am following you; I would like to follow you."

❖ Remembering was this movement of attraction that made her come herself, without any other memory than this indifferent difference.

He was certain that she did not remember, but that she came only in this remembrance, her motionless presence. How could this memory have been shared?

Remembering summoned forgetting as the measure of truth from which he took his leave.

❖ She spoke, going from word to word to use up her presence.

❖ "I did not want you to become attached to my memory. That is why I did not remember myself."*

*The woman says this.

54

❖ "I did not remember myself; that which did remember did not come from me." — "But, as you know, for me you were not a memory. That was even one of our difficulties. You remembered yourself, across from me for whom you remained without a memory." — "And yet I recalled things because you had called me." — "I wanted to help you." — "By wanting to lead me to myself?" — "All I wanted was to help you." — "Yes, a little help does some good." — "I had only a modest role, as you know. I was the wall of this room whose purpose was to send back to you what you would have liked to say." — "A modest role. And yet you waited, you waited all the time." — "I waited," he said, smiling, "I waited to perfection. To know how to wait is the essence of a good wall." — "You waited," she continued. "Except that you couldn't be content just to wait." He was almost in agreement, after thinking it over: "Perhaps; I did what I could. But I did not wish to find my contentment in waiting. Was waiting so serious?" — "It was dreadful." — "And when we weren't there to wait?" — "That was the worst." — "Was it all that bad?" — "It was that bad, as you see me." As he saw her, her face hidden in her hands as if to make her invisible pain more invisible. Yes, as he had to see her.

Her face made more invisible by her invisible suffering.

❖ He asked her: "But don't you have the feeling that I came to look for you here and that I found you? What, then, does all the rest matter?" — "You found me again, perhaps, but without finding me." — "What do you mean?" — "I mean that you do not know whom you found." He took this lightly: "Of course, but that adds to the beauty of the situation. I recognize that you are as unknown to me as you are familiar. It is a wonderful impression." — "She is unknown to you; I am only familiar to you, which you must sense." — "I have a different sense of things. With you, I am on familiar terms with that which is unknown to both of us." —

"I am afraid that this may not be unknown to us in the same way."
— "Why do you say that so sadly?"

❖ For a long time he had believed that the secret counted less than his approach. But here the approach had no approach. He was never closer to or farther from it. Thus, he did not have to approach it; he had only to direct his attention toward it.

❖ "You never address me; you address only this secret in me from which I am separated and which is like my own separation."*

❖ "You have the feeling that you are here secretly. And yet you are here with me." — "If I were not here with you, it would be less secret. The secret is being here with you. And why must we speak of a mystery, a secret? These words horrify me." — "That is true. But we are here to discover what they would like to hide from us." — "There is nothing mysterious; we are making a mystery out of nothing."

When he looked at her, he knew perfectly well that the mystery—a word that she said "horrified" her—was also completely manifest, in this presence that was visible and such that it prevented, by the clarity of that which is only visible, the obscurity of true darkness. However, the presence did not make the mystery present any more than it clarified it. He could not have said that this presence was mysterious; on the contrary, it was devoid of mystery to such an extent that it exposed the mystery without, nevertheless, uncovering it.

❖ Mysterious, that which exposes itself without being uncovered.

❖ And when she spoke about it? Wasn't it mysterious because she spoke about it?

❖ The secret is a burden for him, not because it would ask to

*The female character makes this remark.

be said—that is not possible—but on account of the weight it gives to all the other words, the easiest and lightest ones included, demanding that everything that can be said, with the exception of itself, be said. This enormous necessity for useless words reduces them to equal importance, equal indifference. None of them counts more than the others. What does count is that they all be said equally, in an equality where they are exhausted, without the possibility of saying them being exhausted.

❖ Is it hidden by that which manifests it and makes it manifest?

❖ "Everything that I have not said to you is already forgotten somewhere in you." — "Forgotten, but not in me." — "Also in you." He thought: "I imagine that if it were possible for you to say everything to me, everything that it is possible to say, except this single thing, I would know it in a more definite way than if you had informed me of it directly: it would be delivered to me while remaining free." — "But my life is what you want. I would have to have nothing more to live to have nothing more to say." — "Not exactly your life; on the contrary, it is your life that I am keeping in reserve." — "So, you want more than my life."

❖ "*Act in such a way . . .*" — "Even when you have spoken, it is not certain that you will be aware of it. Perhaps you will only speak to me unaware that you are doing so. You will be delivered by an utterance that you will not be aware of having made to me." — "But you will know that I made it. You will be here to inform me." — "I will be here. What, however, will inform me? How will I learn that this is what I am supposed to hear and if I hear it correctly?" — "In turn, you will make me hear it." — "But it is possible that I will hear silently, as it should be, something that I will not be capable of repeating. And even if I do speak faithfully, you will hear me; you will not hear yourself." She seemed astonished: "You know very well that I must not really hear what I say." Then suddenly: "As soon as you have heard me, I will know: perhaps even before you do." — "Do you mean that you will become aware of this based on my appearance? Will I have changed somehow?" But she repeated joyously: "I will know, I will know."

❖ Speaking, deferring speaking.

Why, when she spoke, did she defer speaking?

The secret—what a crude word—was nothing other than the fact that she spoke and deferred speaking.

If she deferred speaking, this difference kept open the place where, under attraction, the indifferent presence that he had to make visible each time, without letting himself be seen, came.

Letting this indifferent difference come to presence.

❖ "Do that, I ask it of you." — "No, you do not ask it of me."

Silent, a stranger to silence and not silent, this presence.

"Persuade me, even if you do not persuade me." — "But what must I persuade you of?" — "Persuade me."

❖ "Give that to me." — "I cannot give you what I do not have." — "Give that to me." — "I cannot give you that which is not in my power. If I had to, my life, but this thing . . ." — "Give that to me.

"There is no other gift." — "How could I manage it?" — "I don't know. I only know that I ask it of you and that I will ask it of you until the end."

❖ Silent, a stranger to silence and not silent, not speaking, this presence.

How bold she had been in somehow pointing her presence out to him. How slow he had been in understanding this gesture. Now, he understood everything; it was the least that he felt obliged to do. He even understood that it was as if she were frustrated by her presence, frustrated and yet released from herself, not having to remember what she was, but coming only under the attraction of this indifferent difference, her presence. He was ready to move forward in the direction opened up by such a thought, suspecting that if he responded to her presence, he would have to respond to the equal revelation of his presence. But he was still far from such equity.

❖ "Is it here?" — "Of course, if you are here." — "But is it here?"

❖ "This presence." — "Yours." — "Yours also." — "And yet neither the one nor the other."

❖ The secret, this reserve that, if she spoke, caused her to defer speaking, giving her speech in this difference.

"Did I ever promise you that I would speak?" — "No, but it is you who, saying nothing and refusing to say anything and remaining bound to that which is not said, were the promise of speech."

They did not speak; they were the responsive guarantors of every word that was still to be spoken between them.

❖ He has the feeling of waiting less than he waited. This, he thinks, is the sign of the inflation of waiting, a perverse sign.

In waiting, there is always more to await than there are things awaited.

Waiting takes things away from him without his losing them and without his being able to hold on to them through the feeling of having lost them.

He no longer has the strength to wait. If he did, he would not be waiting. He has less strength than he used to, for waiting wears out the strength to wait. Waiting is not worn out. Waiting is a wearing down that is not worn out.*

*Here Blanchot is playing on two different meanings of *usure*: a wearing down or out, and usury. The latter meaning, which I was unable to incorporate here, reinforces the financial metaphor that is initiated in this fragment through the word *majoration*, an increase in price or a surcharge, which I translated as "inflation."

❖ "I hear myself say it constantly." — "That may be why you do not say it. Hearing keeps and takes everything back in itself."

❖ Does he know how to wait? Would he like to extract, by means of this knowing-how-to-wait, the knowledge that belongs to waiting? In that case, he does not know how to wait.

To know how to wait, like a knowledge that could be given only through waiting, provided that one could know how to wait.

❖ Waiting, a road taken by day, one taken by night.

❖ "There is still a long road ahead." — "But not one that will take us far away." — "One that will lead us to what is nearest." — "When everything that is near is farther away than any far-off place."

It is as if she carried the force of proximity in herself. Far away—when she is standing against the door—necessarily close and drawing ever closer, but near to him, still being only close and, nearer, placed completely at a remove by the proximity that she makes manifest. When he holds her, he touches this force of approach that gathers together proximity and, in this proximity, the far-off and the outside in their entirety.

"You are near; she is only present." — "But I am only close, whereas she is presence." — "That is true: only close; I will not deny this 'only,' thanks to which I am holding you here." — "Because you are holding me?" — "Well, you are holding me, too." — "I am holding you. But close to whom?" — "Close: close to everything that is close." — "Close, but not necessarily to you or to me?" — "To neither the one nor the other. But that is how it must be. That is the beauty of attraction: you will never be close enough and never too close; and yet always held and contiguous to each other."

Held and attracted in this contiguity. What attracts is the force of proximity that holds under attraction, without ever being

60

exhausted in presence and dissipated in absence. In proximity, touching not presence, but rather difference.

"Close even if I do not speak?" — "Then letting proximity speak."

What spoke in her was the approach, the approach of speech, speech of the approach, and always approaching speech in speech. "But if I am close, then you are, too." — "Of course. And yet one cannot really say it." — "What can one say?" — "That I am here." — "Whereas I am not really here?" — "You are here, in proximity. That is your privilege; that is the truth of the attraction." The attraction, the manner in which the approach responds to everything by approaching.

"So, we will never cross proximity?" — "But always meeting each other close by."

❖ She is standing against the door, motionless; clearly, she is looking at him. It is perhaps the only moment when he is sure that she ought to discover him, unaware all the same of what the fact of being there signifies for her and how she sees him: a man she vaguely noticed from her balcony a short while ago whom she came to ask, in a movement of rash irritation, the meaning of a gesture about which there is obviously nothing to say. She undoubtedly realizes this at the very moment she enters—apparently without knocking; on this point he will have to question her later, but this kind of politeness would not be consistent with the vehement nature of her movements. One might suppose that irritation was the only motive for her coming, but this is hard to believe. For the moment, she also appears embarrassed, perhaps at the thought of the misunderstanding that such an initiative, which was difficult to justify and at the very least surprising, could give rise to. Whence the surprise, the most obvious feature of her presence, the one that would disconcert him if the calm assurance of youth had not already prepared him to see nothing extraordinary in this coming.

The surprise is visible: she took over the anger so well that it seemed to converge with the abrupt and closed aspect of the surprise, whether she feels the surprise or manifests it, in her surprising presence, surprising also for the very reason that it displaces every other presence, to the extent that he is the one who should feel like an intruder in this room that he momentarily shares with her. This impression of intrusion barely crosses his mind. Far from thinking about surrendering his place to her, he experiences the cold jubilation of the hunter when the trap has worked and hands over, in a now certain proximity, the awaited prey. The idea that she is there and that he will not let her leave is, therefore, almost the only one that must occupy him at this moment.

The room is fairly long and abnormally narrow, which he had already noticed; but this narrowness of a room with slightly sloping, attic-like walls gives it the appearance of a corridor, as a result of this presence at one of its extremities, a presence that accentuates the imbalance of the dimensions.

She seems well acquainted with the room because when she enters it—probably without knocking and so abruptly that it is he who has the impression of having entered her room and of catching her by surprise in this motionless attitude, astonished, embarrassed, indignant—she does not look around, not even fleetingly (as anyone arriving in an unfamiliar place cannot fail to do), but rather stares precisely in the only direction that is important for her to be facing: toward him. This is natural. Provided that she has indeed come to see him, and not for other reasons that still escape him and that would justify her conduct in a more satisfactory way: if, for example, she had seized on this pretext to gain entrance to this room to which she was attached by the memory of some previous episode, which would explain the impression of familiarity, of intimacy, but also of disaccord that he thinks he discerned between her and her surroundings. It might be that his presence, the sign he addressed to her, the advances he made to her, had suddenly awakened a past to whose attraction she submitted before controlling it, or, more simply, perhaps it was a mistake, and from afar she took him for someone she had already met but who, she realizes now, is not the person she thought him to be, although he shares with this person qualities that are so disturbing that they prevent the error from being recognized as such. Naturally, he is free to believe that by responding to his invitation in a seemingly mechanical and obligatory way, she is merely complying with the customary usage of the place, if it is true, as he has reason to believe, that a section of the hotel is reserved for such comings and goings. This idea does not displease him.

❖ When he had said to her: "Come"—and immediately she approaches slowly, not in spite of herself, but with a simplicity that does not make her presence closer—shouldn't he have gone to meet her instead of formulating this imperious invitation? But perhaps he was afraid of frightening her with his gesture; he wants to let her be free, and if she is not free in her initiative, at least free in her movement. (She chooses a very slow movement, the one most foreign to hesitation for the very reason of its slowness, movement in which the immobility that is particular to it and that contrasts with the brevity of the authoritarian invitation is held back.) So, it is an authoritarian word? — But also an intimate one. — A violent word. — But one carrying only the violence of a word. — Carrying it far. — Reaching the far-off without harming it. — With this word, doesn't he wrest the violence from the far-off? — He left it there. The violence is, therefore, still at the farthest possible distance? — But it is the farthest distance that is close.[*]

The word is only the extension of the sign he made to her. The sign, in enduring, is changed into a word of appeal necessarily

---

[*]This is one of two instances in the text where there is a dialogue without quotation marks. The other occurrence is found in one of the last fragments of the book, beginning "They went, motionless, . . ."

pronounced in a low and impersonal tone of voice in which the attraction of the expanse is affirmed. But did the sign say anything? It made a sign by designating. But is the appeal more demanding? It goes toward that to which it appeals. But does it make something come? Only that which asks to come in the appeal. But is it an appeal that questions? It responds by appealing.

❖ How would it be possible to harm the simplicity of presence?

❖ If that which escapes waiting is always already present in waiting, everything is given, save the simplicity of presence.

Waiting is the awaiting of presence that is not given in waiting, presence that is led, however, to the simple play of presence by waiting that withdraws from presence everything that is present in it.

❖ It is as if they still had to look for the road that would take them to where they already are.

❖ She let his remark pass and insisted: "Since I said it to you. But it was undoubtedly too simple." — "It was wonderfully simple." — "Too simple to be able to be said." — "But said on account of simplicity."

❖ He has the impression of seeing her less than he does of seeing her approach, seizing in her through a feeling that is strange in its scope the power of the approach that is uniquely hers.

❖ "When you approached . . ." — "Why are you speaking in the past tense?" — "Because it's easier; the words want to speak in the past." — "I know; I have always known that you do not wish to compromise this presence. Where is she now?"* — "Well, over there where you are. But I could also say: sitting on the sofa, her body turned slightly away, her head somewhat lowered, as if she

*The implied existence of a second woman, to which I referred in a previous note, becomes explicit in this fragment and others that follow.

64

were leaning." — "So, she is no longer turned toward you?" — "No, not exactly." — "Why are you so imprecise?" And suddenly: "But where are you?" — "I think that I came over to sit next to her, but a little behind, since she is at the end of the sofa, and close enough so that I can touch her shoulders, which the bowed nape of her neck leaves exposed." — "I see. You are going to make her slip and in this way pull her gradually against yourself?" — "Perhaps; it is a natural movement." — "But isn't it cowardly? She cannot resist like that." — "Why would she resist? Everything has been played out for a long time. Do you have any reason for advancing this point of view?" — "What point of view?" — "The idea that she would like things to stay where they are." — "Of course she doesn't want that. However, why is she turned like that, almost turned away? You have to admit that her attitude is not one of simple consent." — "This is true; I admit it. But that is her way of responding to the attraction, neither refusing nor accepting, through a simplicity that has always already rendered useless the difference between these ways of acting." — "And yet everything is not said." — "Nothing is said."

"At what moment did you decide to go over there?" — "To the sofa?" — "Yes." — "When I saw her sitting there." — "Waiting for you?" — "Waiting for me, not waiting for me." — "And weren't you afraid of startling her?" — "That didn't even occur to me; I acted very quickly." — "Yes, you are quick. And when she noted your presence?" As he did not answer: "Didn't she stiffen when you took hold of her shoulders?" — "Well, you know, the contact was very slight, simply a manner of suggesting to her that I was there and that from then on we had all the time we needed." — "Yes, this impression that distances have all of a sudden disappeared and that the story can only follow its course is pleasant. But don't you think that you exhibited too much assurance? Weren't you too sure of yourself?" — "One might think so. These things are necessarily done because of excessive assurance." — "You didn't know her;

you didn't know why she had come." — "I didn't know why, but I did nothing except ask her why." — "Just like that?" — "Ah, she is more simple than you.

"And do not forget that during the entire time, the remarkable impression of a wonderful force of approach was given to me: everything depended on that." — "Someone unknown can also approach." — "Absolutely, and even only that which is unknown; that is what makes it wonderful. I had the impression that I was more unknown to her than to any other person I have met until now." — "Is that why you concluded that you could proceed unabashedly?" — "Someone who doesn't know you at all and whom no one knows at all: this is what is pleasant about these encounters. But there was something else." — "Which is?" — "Well, that is difficult to say. She made it easy for herself to be watched." — "Indeed! Do you mean that she willingly made a spectacle of herself?" — "I wouldn't say that. If it is true that a certain spectacular impression is prevalent—but one that is very diluted, rarefied, a spectacle that would take place in an area that I would not be obliged to watch over—she does not participate in it; on the contrary, she may even be frustrated by it." — "Weren't you really looking at her rather in a carefree way?" — "Perhaps, but through a carefree detachment that came from her: yes, without caring about whether I had the right to look at her."

As if to look were not only linked to the application of the ability to look but were rooted in the affirmation of her presence already so exposed and still hidden.

"Why does she let herself be seen like this?" — "She does it out of pleasure, I imagine, the pleasure of being visible." — "And yet never visible enough." — "Naturally, never visible enough."

❖ Standing against the door, motionless and always approaching, while seated at the far end of the sofa, her body turned slightly away, lying down, leaning back against him, slipping, and he, letting her slip backward, making her traverse, through the expanse where she is leaning back, the portion of space, uncrossable and already crossed, that separates her, her face passing before him, while she falls, her eyes peacefully open, as if they were meant to see each other, even if there is no reason for them to look at each other.

As he takes hold of her, imperceptibly surrounding her such as she will be and attracting her with a still unaccomplished movement of attraction, she slips, an image in this slipping, slipping into her image.

❖ "Yes, I know, it was already her manner of struggling against her presence." — "Oh, she doesn't struggle." — "It's true; she understood wonderfully that she must neither resist nor consent but rather slip, suspended, between the two, motionless in her haste and her slowness." — "She does nothing except respond to you." — "But no more to me than to anyone else." — "To you as to no one: that is what is extremely attractive." — "Thus attracted as if out of her presence." — "Attracted, but nevertheless not yet, through the attraction of that which always attracts, but not yet." — "Through the attraction that forces, rejects, and occupies all distance." — "Attracted in her, in this place of attraction that she feels herself become." — "Present everywhere." — "Present without presence." — "Present through this surplus of heaviness and lightness that is the gift she gives to space and that makes her equal to the entire expanse where she leans back." — "Leaning back against him." — "Slipping into her." — "Given to the outside." — "Leaning back and showing herself through a passion of appearing that turns her away from everything visible and invisible."

❖ When she sat up ever so slightly, without putting any distance between them, propping herself up instead at an angle as if to push away, out of peaceful necessity, their two reclining bodies, she said: "Does she say that a short time later?" — "A short time later, if you wish." — "Is she still close to you?" — "She is sitting up ever so slightly." — "So that she can look at you better?" — "Perhaps so that she can breathe easier." — "And she isn't looking at you?" — "She is looking rather at what she says."

❖ That which has been accomplished asks for its accomplishment.

❖ "How did they happen to speak to each other?" This made her laugh: "Isn't it natural?" — "I think it is, too; and yet I believe that there was another reason and that because of this reason, whatever made their words natural also made them very difficult. Otherwise, why would he have been suddenly surprised to hear her? And why was he certain that by entrusting to him what was still only her voice, a somewhat weak but also distinct and cold voice, she demanded of him a trust to which he succeeded in responding only with difficulty, in spite of his attention?" — "This is bound to happen early on." — "This happened on that occasion, at least."

❖ "What in these words surprises you? They are simple." — "I think that I had gotten used to the idea that you would not speak. You still hadn't said anything so far, and there wasn't anything to say, either." — "And you thought that things had gotten to the point where they would withdraw and not be expressed? What is in this voice that was more unexpected than anything that happened and that you profited from so easily?" — "Nothing more. Only a little less. There is—this is the voice's role—suddenly less than there was: this is what the surprise consists of." — "And it is because of the voice? Do you reproach it for some reason?" — "There is nothing to reproach it for. It is a somewhat weak, slightly veiled voice: perhaps more distinct or colder than I would have expected." — "You are reticent; you should be more frank. Is there something strange about it?" — "It is as familiar as a voice can be. Could it be its tranquil reality that surprises me by abruptly withdrawing some of the reality from the other things?" — "The other things? Everything that happened?" — "They, too, have their reality, naturally, but it may be that everything that seemed so simple to me so far is suddenly coming up against another simplicity that is somehow affirmed in the voice. Something is changing."

The surprise that is the retreat of things and also of surprising things.

That the voice is all of a sudden placed there, one thing among others, adding only the element of disclosure that even such a simple encounter does not seem to be able to do without, this abrupt appearance surprises him, and while she speaks in an almost direct manner, putting herself completely into each word and keeping nothing in reserve so as to say something more, she has already acceded to other levels where she is ready to make herself heard or has already necessarily expressed herself, filling in time, ahead, behind, the entire void, as she fills all the silence in the room, in spite of her weak ability, which is sometimes withdrawn, sometimes outside, always distant and always close, searching and specifying, as if being precise were the principal safeguard of this voice that says, somewhat coldly: "I would like to speak to you."

❖ He searches, turning around and around with, in the center, this speech and knowing that to find is merely to continue to search through the relation to the center, which is unlocatable. The center makes finding and turning possible but cannot be found in and of itself. The center as center is always intact.

Turning around her presence, which he could encounter only in this turning away.

The view of her (turned-away) presence directly across from him.

❖ "What are you thinking about?" — "This thought that must not be thought."

The closest thought, the one that must not be thought.

There is a thought that must not be thought. Not to think it would suffice for the negation under which he is placed to be accomplished. Impossible to think? Forbidden to thought? A familiar thought, it is one among others and is waiting not to be thought. Not thinking it even as the one that must not be thought. Living under the pressure exerted by that which stays there unthought.

"There is a thought that I am unable to think." — "And you would like to tell it to me so that I will try to think it?" — "So that you will not be able to think it."

"Why would we be closer in this thought?" — "Because it displaces all proximity."

❖ When she had said that to him, and since he was barely attentive and did not seem surprised, she had wanted to repeat it, but it was to no avail. Later on, in spite of all his efforts to get her to say it again, she was never able to find the expression that she had used in the course of that sentence or those two sentences. It was, she said, part of a larger scheme of things, one that had literally been dismantled, and all that remained was the emptiness of the request in his presence.

It has nothing to do with her refusing or being embarrassed to talk about it; on the contrary, she is only too willing to talk about it: lightly, unknowingly, passionately.

"Saying it again is easy, but saying it again a first time?" — "That would be easy if you hadn't begun by saying it again."

He understands that she can ask only by using turns and detours of time. But it is a request—this, too, he understands—that can only present itself, and in such a direct manner that there is no time to maintain it.

The request is hidden and hides the immediacy of the request in the detours of waiting, detours that do not qualify as intermediaries. There is nothing except the request that requests immediately and the waiting that submits to it through waiting. Speech goes from one to the other without acting as a mediator.

❖ "Let's wait; you will certainly speak eventually." — "Waiting does not give speech." — "But speech responds to waiting."

The words conveyed by speech conveyed by the voice restrained by waiting.

In each word, not words but the space that, appearing, disappearing, they designate as the moving space of their appearance and their disappearance.

In each word, a response to the unexpressed, the refusal and attraction of the unexpressed.

"We are no longer waiting; we shall wait no longer." — "Actually, we never really waited." — "So, has it all been for naught? So many wasted efforts, so many arrested moments?" — "We were patient and motionless." — "And mustn't I still tell you everything?" — "It is not necessary, now, for us to speak. Let us remain peacefully hearing each other."

❖ In waiting where there is no longer anything that can differ. Waiting is difference that has already taken back everything different. Indifferent, it carries difference.

The perpetual coming and going of waiting: its cessation. The motionlessness of waiting, moving more than any movement.

Waiting is always hidden in waiting. Whoever waits enters the hidden trait of waiting.

That which is hidden opens itself to waiting, not to be discovered, but rather to remain hidden there.

Waiting neither opens nor closes. The entering into a relation that neither welcomes nor excludes. Waiting is foreign to the self-concealing/self-revealing movement of things.

Nothing is hidden to anyone who waits. Whoever waits is not in the company of things that reveal themselves. In waiting, all things are returned toward the latent state.

❖ He is no longer protected by the hidden aspect of things.

❖ Waiting: attracted by waiting in this interval between seeing and saying that he only endures thanks to the story and where the latter plays itself out while displaying its hand, but immediately—and perhaps from the beginning—rejected by the truth of the story's game toward waiting that keeps the two of them as if they were at a remove from presence.

"We have moved a long distance away." — "Together." — "But also from each other." — "And also from ourselves." — "Distancing makes no concessions." — "Distancing distances in distancing." — "And thus brings us close together." — "But far from us."

Even if she waits mysteriously for the end to come to her as the gift of his death, she awaits it from the story that she cannot tell him about and, in the story, she cannot evoke this gift that she awaits, either; always waiting to acquire it thanks to this story that he should accept to take up at the level of words that have come from him and finding then their meaning in the use of his death to come.

"What keeps them separated, displacing both of them from presence . . ." — "is the story where she attracts him and where there can be no presence except that which is expressed." — "Presence that is always intact, only present through the detour of the story." — "But what allows the story to unfold as the calm play of the story . . ." — "is this gap where they are both already waiting, removed from presence. . . ." — "And in this gap, in the void between seeing and saying, carried illegitimately toward each other through waiting." — "Through forgetting."

Waiting, a road taken by day and by night, is the way that leads from the event she awaits to the story where she awaits it, both of which are kept together by forgetting: the detour that he makes and where he remains, exposed to things when, neither hidden nor manifest, they return to the latent state, and the same applies to her, whether he likes it or not, in the relation he maintains with her, and the same applies to him in the relation she maintains with him.

"But we are here to keep the secret." — "Unless the secret is keeping us." — "And we are here: that is the entire secret." — "Yes, but are we here?" — "That is the entire secret." — "And the fact that we are here secretly." — "Secretly and manifestly." — "Secretly in this manifestation." — "This is our superiority over them: as if we were their secret." — "But they do not have a secret." — "They don't know that; they believe that there is one." — "But we know better." — "Yes, we know better."

And yet the following moment, stopping and looking: "But this presence."

Going toward the presence, toward which they are not able to go. They are brought back, however, by it to everything that comes, and thus they are turned toward it. Always turned farther away in this detour.

"Why do you want to awaken from this presence that you speak to me about?" — "Perhaps so that I will fall asleep in this awakening. More than that, I don't know if I want this, and you don't, either; you may not." — "How could I? Where I am, there is nothing I am capable of wanting. I wait. This is my role within waiting, going toward waiting." — "Waiting, waiting, what a strange word!"

"Where do they wait? Here or outside?" — "Here, which keeps them outside." — "In the place where they speak or the place about which they speak?" — "The force of waiting, maintained in its truth, is to lead, wherever one is waiting, to the place of waiting." — "In secret, without a secret?" — "In secret in sight of everyone."

"And did death come quickly?" — "Very quickly. But dying is long."

Speaking instead of dying.

Immortal in the instant of dying on account of their being closer to death than mortals: present to death.

"They are incapable of dying, for lack of a future." — "Granted, but they are no more capable of being present." — "They are not present; of them, there is only the presence where they disappear slowly, eternally." — "A presence with no one, perhaps." — "A presence where they disappear, the presence of the disappearance." — "Forgetting, forgotten." — "Forgetting has no hold over presence." — "Presence that does not belong to remembrance."

❖ What made him believe that it was as if he had lost the idea of dying? Yes, what made him believe this? The feeling that he is looking for it? He is looking for it! In this case, even if he finds it, he will still have found only an idea. Nevertheless, an idea of a particular kind.

It is as if he were suddenly ignorant of more things than he could be ignorant of. He must look for the center of gravity of this ignorance, not in ill-suited words such as *death* and *life*, but rather here where he remains: in a state of waiting between seeing and saying.

To see, to forget to speak; to speak, to exhaust in the depths of speech forgetting, the inexhaustible.

This void between seeing and saying, where they are carried illegitimately toward each other.

When he asks himself where this gift of ignorance comes to him from, a gift that does not bring him, except when he avoids it, any dizziness, confusion, or feelings of power or powerlessness but rather waiting in its peacefulness, he should respond: it comes from having captured, starting from simplicity mysteriously unfolded, the play between presence that is seen, even if it is not seen, and presence that gives rise to speech. It is a separation that isn't one, a split nonetheless, but one that does not let itself be perceived and that is not really denounced, since it is supposed to introduce an interval between the visible/invisible and the sayable/unsayable. There where, according to the general law, a perfect suture hides the secret of the joining together, the secret here, in the manner of a tear, shows itself in its hidden aspect. Of this void, in accordance with their respective paths, they are both witnesses.* It is, he believes, the place of ignorance and attention. It is, but she does not say it, the heart of presence, this heart that she would perhaps like him to wound with a violent gift.

As if, suddenly, ignorant of more than he is capable of being ignorant of . . .

He senses strongly that the idea of dying has been pulled into this ignorance, and when, through a certain slippage of words, she suggests to him, as she grapples painfully with things she does not know, that she seems deprived of an end and that if she had to die, she could do so only by dying his death, this thought appears to him to belong to the play of ignorance that occurs between speech and presence.

He speaks of this; speech does not betray ignorance.

❖ At one moment, he had said cheerfully to her, "Oh, you are mysterious." To which she had replied, not without bitterness, "Why would I be mysterious when I have, on the contrary, slightly distanced myself from all mystery?"

❖ If the thing were separated into the thing that is seen and the thing that is said, speech would work on eliminating this separation, on making it more profound, on leaving it intact while making it speak, on disappearing in it. But this separation that speech works on is still only a separation in speech. Unless there is speech on

---

*In this sentence, Blanchot exploits the identical pronunciation of *voies*, which I have rendered as "paths," and *voix* (voices). The same play on words reappears four fragments farther along.

account of this separation, speaking in an always separated speech. Also on account of the simplicity of presence, simplicity that is in itself the simplicity of that which is seen and that which is said.

Presence is not only separated; it is what still comes at the heart of the separation.

Little by little, the question that he had always held back: "How could she have distanced herself from her presence?" was lost in this answer: "There is nothing mysterious about it; the secret would be, rather, the point where the distance happens to cease. This point—in the delineated void between seeing and saying—escapes whoever sees it and whoever says it."

The mystery—what a crude word—would be the point where the thing that is seen and the thing that is said meet in the simplicity of presence. A mystery that could be grasped only if it separates itself, by a slight oscillation, from the mysterious point.

❖ "What is this idea that you would like me to keep?" — "You are here and you are keeping it: this is what is necessary." — "Like a treasure?" — "Like the fire of ancient days."

❖ "It is true that I am ignorant of many things about you." — "To the point of being ignorant of me." — "Oh, ignorance is our path, and yet we struggle valiantly to lessen it." — "Yes, we do struggle." He reflects: "I am not ignorant of you; it would be a mistake to think that. I am not ignorant of you in particular." — "Do you mean that ignorance does no harm to our relations?" — "I don't even mean that. Ignorance relates us to each other, as if I had to see you and speak to you by way of the detour of excessive ignorance." — "Something that you are ignorant of?" — "Is it something?" — "That does not let itself be said?" — "Or seen, but rather at the intersection of the two. It is in the vicinity of everything that occurs, with no possibility of its occurring." — "And is it here all the same?" — "How can it be said?"

❖ He sees her, if he sees her, through ignorance.

The gaze borne by waiting. A gaze inclined toward that which turns away from everything visible and invisible. Waiting gives the gaze time to traverse ignorance.

❖ "I never questioned you." — "And yet you took hold of me and immobilized me with questions, and it was as though you deprived me of an end." — "No, I did not question you." — "You attracted me in the midst of things to say."

❖ That she ceases to be mysterious is perhaps an enigma, still a mystery, but a passing one, the moment when, not abandoning their former resources, they persist in speaking as if to speak were still to see. But he cannot welcome, except as a secret that concerns both of them, the manner in which they are approached by the event through which, in a present of the future or past, she lifts herself up fortuitously and lightly out of all mystery, an event erected like a monument of forgetting, ignorance, and waiting, like her own presence (forgotten, unknown, awaited), at the center of this space of speech.

While she lifts herself up out of all mystery, he believes that he sees her thanks to this mystery that fades from her, but what he sees is himself being submerged by it, at the moment he would like to make the move to distinguish himself from it.

❖ "I will see you better when we have forgotten to speak." — "But if I did not forget, I would not speak." — "That is true: it is as though you speak through forgetting; speaking, forgetting to speak." — "Speech is given to forgetting."

"What is important is not that you remember or forget but rather that remembering, you remain faithful to forgetting in the space from which you remember and, forgetting, faithful to the coming that makes you remember."

❖ The event that they forget: the event of forgetting. And thus, all the more present insofar as it is forgotten. Giving forgetting and giving itself forgotten, but not being forgotten. Presence of forgetting and in forgetting. The ability to forget endlessly in the event that is forgotten. Forgetting without the possibility of forgetting. Forgetting-forgotten without forgetting.

Forgotten presence is always vast and deep. The depth of forgetting in presence.

"You, too, forgot me."* — "Perhaps, but in forgetting you, I reached an ability to forget you that far exceeds my understanding and that links me, well beyond me, to what I forget. It is almost too much for one person." — "You are not alone." — "Yes, I am not the only one who forgets, if I forget."

Words seemingly forgotten before they are said, always wending their way toward forgetting, unforgettable.

"If you have forgotten what I said, that is good. It was said for forgetting."

❖ In the room: when he turns back toward the time he made a sign to her, he feels that he makes a sign to her in turning back. And if she comes and he takes hold of her, in an instant of freedom about which there is nothing to say and that he has long since wondrously forgotten, he owes the initiative to which her presence responds to the power of forgetting (and to the necessity of speech) that this instant grants him.

"I do not remember." — "But you come." — "While moving away." — "You come closer in this moving away." — "Remaining motionless." — "You are at rest through the strong attraction of the movement." — "Restless rest."

❖ Never any sleep between them, even if they sleep. He accepted that long ago.

❖ She sat up slightly, leaning to the side on her hand. She was then next to the wall and seemed to rise up above their two reclining

*The woman is speaking here.

bodies, looking at both of them and saying in a voice whose cold clearness surprised him: "I would like to speak to you. When could I do that?" — "Can you spend the night here?" — "Yes." — "Can you stay as of now?" — "Yes."

While he listens to this "yes," wondering if she really pronounced it (it is so transparent that it lets what she says, including this very word, pass through), she leans back as if she were already delivered, while taking care not to put any distance between them.

He attracts her, attracted by the attraction in his as yet unaccomplished movement. But while she rises up in the one he is touching, and although he knows that she is slipping, falling, a motionless figure, he does not stop marking out a path for her and leading her, pressing forward, as she holds onto him tightly in a movement that renders them indistinguishable.

She speaks, spoken rather than speaking, as if her own speech passed through her alive and painfully transformed her into the space of another kind of speech, always interrupted, lifeless.

And most certainly, when in the morning light—undoubtedly they have just awakened together—he hears her ask fervently, "Could I have spoken without stopping?" he does not doubt being invited to take possession, in this single sentence, of everything that she said to him during the night.

❖ He discerns this even speech that he hears at the limit of everything she says, but to discern it is already to make it different, to force it in its indifference.

This even speech that he hears: neither close by nor far away, not giving space and not letting things be situated in space, even, but not even with anything, always different in its indifference, and having never come, preventing all coming, preventing all presence, and yet always said, although hidden in the simplicity of what it says. How could he take it back to her?

Listening to this even speech whose truth he is asked to maintain, through attention, at the limit of waiting, by responding to it.

❖ "Does that come to pass?" — "No, it does not."

❖ Pain like used-up, forgotten speech, occupying each day, each night.

What she says, as he is well aware, is directed toward this even speech that she does not cease saying at the limit of waiting. Thus speaking, forbidden. And yet, with the patience that is particular to him, he thinks that if he could, by responding to her, elicit from her the measureless evenness of the murmur and master it, a kind of measure of evenness would be established between their words that would be capable of making more expressive and more silent, to the point of pacifying it, the incessant affirmation.

Something in her affirms gently, evenly, without limits, without stopping: it is gentle and attractive; it attracts unceasingly. When she speaks, the words let themselves gently slip toward the affirmation, and she, too, seems to slip there, attractive, attracted, keeping silent, not keeping silent. It is as if she were furtively withdrawing, even as she lets herself be held.

❖ "Does that come to pass?" — "No, it does not."

❖ He listens at a distance to what they say to each other, a distance that their words themselves accord him so that they can be heard. Between these words, no accord, no discord, but rather (and this touches him painfully) the calm search for an even measure. Always distinct and yet equivalent, speaking beside this evenness, speaking in view of that which must make them even.

Their words are not yet even with each other, even if they say what relates them evenly to each other.

As if their words were searching for the level where, even with each other, they would allow the silent evenness, the one that comes to light in the end, to be established between them.

Speech of sand, murmur of the wind.

❖ "Does that come to pass?" — "No, it does not." — "Something, however, is coming."

❖ Elation, this pure movement of elevation that transports them both, in considerate speech, toward that which turns away.

❖ In the place where they were, still looking for some relation that would bind them to each other. Even without words, even without movement, always speaking, always moving, and imperceptibly desiring each other without desire.

"What has become of the story?" — "There must not be much of the story left at present."

❖ He remembers that she stays there motionless, and while he helps her remove some of her clothing without breaking with the motionlessness, not waiting for her to stop speaking to him and himself saying to her: what do you remember at the present time? he attracts her, takes hold of her, lets his gaze play over her face, as she lets herself slip, her eyes calmly open, motionless presence turned away from presence. Only her hand, one that she docilely abandoned to him, is still withheld, warm and fidgety, like a little, smooth creature stirring in its search for food.

The room before him: narrow and long, abnormally long perhaps, such that it extends far to the outside, in a strictly delimited space, although insufficiently specified, with fixed points of reference. Two windows form oblique openings in the wall, the black expanse of a table on which he thinks he writes, the chair where she remains seated, upright, her hands idle, or she is over there, standing against the door. Next to him, on the sofa, is the body of the young woman that is slightly turned away, while he remembers that she spoke to him late into the night.

❖ "Yes, you spoke to me very much; you were infinitely generous." — "Is that true? Could you attest to this?" — "I can attest to it, I will attest to it as much as you like." — "That cannot be. Think. That would be worse than everything else. Act in such a way that I can speak to you." — "Well, rest assured that you spoke to me more than I heard you." — "So, I spoke, and I did so in vain. That is the worst."

❖ This even speech that he hears: evenness that if it were light in the daylight, tension in attention, would be justice in death.

"Of all the ones to whom I spoke, I spoke only to him, and if I spoke with others, it is only because of him or in relation to him or in the forgetting of him." — "If this is the case, it is indeed with me that you are speaking now."

This even speech, spaced without space, affirming beneath all affirmation, impossible to deny, too weak to be silenced, too docile to be contained, not saying something, only speaking, speaking without life, without a voice, in a voice lower than any other: living among the dead, dead among the living, calling to die, to come back to life in order to die, calling without appeal.

He attempts to lead this even speech, while letting himself be led by it, toward this measure of evenness, light in the daylight, tension in attention, justice in death.

He knows that waiting participates in such a measure: in waiting entering the evenness of waiting, even if waiting always exceeds waiting in its evenness with itself.

❖ "When your words are at the same level as mine, when they are equal in this way, they will no longer speak." — "Undoubtedly, but between them the silent evenness will be withheld."

❖ In a low voice for himself, in a lower voice for him. Inconsequential speech that he follows, nowhere-wandering, everywhere-residing. The necessity of letting it go.

Speech in flight that they follow.

She is fleeing and borne by her flight toward the one she is fleeing from, whereas ignorant of her, supporting her, he stays close to her a few long paces away, already almost turning back like a traitor, but faithfully.

❖ "He attracted me, he attracted me constantly." — "Where did he attract you?" — "Well, into this thought that I have forgotten." — "And can you remember him better?" — "I cannot. How I have forgotten him. How he attracts me, the one whom I have forgotten."

❖ When she speaks and her words are gently pulled along, her face slipping in turn, plunging into the flow of even speech, she also attracts him in this same movement of attraction where she does not know whom she is following, who precedes her.

As if he had slipped, through the attraction of the measureless affirmation, toward this empty space where, leading her, following her, he remains suspended between seeing and saying.

❖ The night like a unique word, the word *end* repeated endlessly.*

❖ This even speech that he hears, unique without unity, the murmur of one alone as of a multitude, carrying forgetting, hiding forgetting.

An affirmation that attracts all words while turning them away.

"Does that come to pass?" — "No, it does not." — "Something comes, however." — "In waiting that stops and leaves all coming behind." — "Something comes, coming outside waiting." — "Waiting is the calm leaving behind that leaves in its future everything that comes."

❖ That she waited for the event of the story itself, where she would have liked, through the truth of the words chosen by him, to arrive at an end for which he would have been so responsible

*_Le mot fin_ (the word *end*) can also be understood as "the subtle word."

83

that it would have represented the gift of his death, is what he learned through waiting, trying to turn her away from this end through waiting, through forgetting.

❖ He asked her: "Do you suffer?" — "No, I do not. There is only this suffering behind me that I do not suffer."

He asked her in a lower voice: "But do you suffer?" — "When you ask me like that, I feel that later, much later, I could suffer."

❖ They went, motionless, letting presence come. — Which, however, does not come. — Which, however, never already came. — From which, however, comes any future. — In which, however, every present disappears.

"Which way does the road go?" — "Through your entrusted body, which is covered in this final journey."

The affront of presence. Confronted with space and presence.

It is a slow movement where, absorbed in what she says, slipping, falling in what she says, she lets herself be carried by the dispersal of speech in her, and pressed tightly against him, walking in his footsteps at the same pace, while he carries her, takes hold of her, avidly perusing her, not waiting for her to stop speaking so that he can make her silent.

"I am afraid; I remember fear." — "That doesn't matter; have confidence in your fear." And they continued to move forward.

How motionless he is, the one whom she is following.

How little you speak, you who are the last to make a sign.

"When I am before you and would like to look at you, to speak to you . . ." — *"He takes hold of her and attracts her, drawing her out of her presence."* — *"When I approach, motionless, my pace bound to your pace, calm, hurried . . ."* — *"She leans back against him, holding back, letting herself go."* — *"When you go ahead, marking out a path for me to you . . ."* — *"She slips, rising up in the one he touches."* — *"When we come and go in the room and look for an instant at . . ."* — *"She holds back in her, drawn back outside her, waiting for what happened to happen."* — *"When we move away from each other, and also from ourselves, and thus approach each other, but far from each other . . ."* — *"That is the coming and going of waiting: its cessation."* — *"When we remember and forget, reunited: separated . . ."* — *"That is the motionlessness of waiting: in motion more than any movement."* — *"But when you say: 'Come,' and I come to this place of attraction . . ."* — *"She falls, given to the outside, her eyes calmly open."* — *"When you turn back and make me a sign . . ."* — *"She turns away from everything visible and invisible."* — *"Leaning back and showing herself."* — *"Face to face in this calm turning away."* — *"Not here where she is or here where he is, but between them."* — *"Between them, like this place, with its great staring look, the reserve of things in their latent state."*

André Breton
The Lost Steps
Translated by Mark Polizzotti

André Breton
Mad Love
Translated by Mary Ann Caws

In the French Modernist Library series

Louis Aragon
The Adventures of Telemachus
Translated by Renée Riese Hubert
and Judd D. Hubert

Louis Aragon
Treatise on Style
Translated by Alyson Waters

Marcel Bénabou
*Why I Have Not Written Any
of My Books*
Translated by David Kornacker

Maurice Blanchot
Awaiting Oblivion
Translated by John Gregg

Maurice Blanchot
The Most High
Translated by Allan Stoekl

André Breton
Communicating Vessels
Translated by Mary Ann Caws
and Geoffrey T. Harris

André Breton
Free Rein
Translated by Michel Parmentier
and Jacqueline d'Amboise

Blaise Cendrars
Modernities and Other Writings
Edited by Monique Chefdor
Translated by Esther Allen and
Monique Chefdor

The Cubist Poets in Paris: An Anthology
Edited by L. C. Breunig

René Daumal
You've Always Been Wrong
Translated by Thomas Vosteen

Max Jacob
Hesitant Fire: Selected Prose of Max Jacob
Translated and edited by Moishe Black
and Maria Green

Jean Paulhan
Progress in Love on the Slow Side
Translated by Christine Moneera
Laennec and Michael Syrotinski

Benjamin Péret
Death to the Pigs, and Other Writings
Translated by Rachel Stella and Others

Boris Vian
Blues for a Black Cat and Other Stories
Edited and translated by Julia Older